Loggers Don't Make Love

by Dave Rowan

Published by
Cirque Press

CIRQUE PRESS

Sandra Kleven — Michael Burwell
3157 Bettles Bay Loop
Anchorage, AK 99515

cirquejournal@gmail.com
www.cirquejournal.com

Cover Art by David Danioth and Author
Cover Design by Janna Christen

ISBN: 978-1-0879-0509-9

Make it a banger. People don't want to hear the truth. They live in their dreams. Change all the names. Give them all funny ones, like Rigging Red. I once knew a guy named that. He was a rigger. He was a hell of a man. He liked to stand on top of the tree after he topped it and take a piss. One day it got him. He fell off and died with his pecker in his hand.

—Carl Stumps
   in a bar in
   Shelton

In Memory of

Jes Searcy, Dale Green, Bob Cooper and Ken Frazier

And Dedicated

to all the men and women who walked the planks of Grisdale, especially the ones I still remember, many who are dead now, too:

Bob Honeywell, Carl Shores, Robert Fudge, Steve Russell, Mike Kinley, Frank Gwyn, Dennis Green, Bill Cather, Chuck Mitman, Terry Brown, Tom Smith, Vic Del, Ralph Christwell, Wayne Arrington, Gary Hurleman, Jack Walker, Jack Wilson (who served in WWII with my father), Kenny Howard, Mike Norwood, Chet Swearingen, Ray Bowles, Doug Kingery, Mark Trails, Jim Huston, Tom Maguire, Tracy Ridout, Jes Ferrier, Elmer Ferrier, Jim Compton, Don Gamburg, Chuck Pulcifer, Gary White, Chuck Bingham, Terry Sizemore, Tom Oin, Mary, Mike Sliffer, Earl Neal, Paul Kunkel, Max Durwood, Charlie Alexander, Terry Feldon, Ralph Canady, John Anderson, Jim Vanhorn, Buck, JT, Jim Churchill, Rob Becker, George, Claude, Doggy Dale, Bunny, Dan Mildridge, Leo Figurito, Zigy Kaluzny, Mike Smith, Bill Goldsmith, Bill Shearer, Bill Clark, Ernie Stilar, Carl Stumps, Orrel Ostrander, Mark Moody, Daisy, Mark Munday, the rest of the Greens, all the Grahams, all the Brehmeyers, all the Corcorans, Warren Turner, Betty & Jim Jones, Leah & Steve Lawerman, Roger Hanson, Kieth Byrd, Jerry Barnhart, Bud Dietrich & Storm, Little Cathie & the camp girls & boys, and Irene. With special thanks to Ken Marshall, Rich Miller and Bob Hammond who taught me how to log at Govey.

Also By Dave Rowan

Around the Edge of the Olympics on a Mountain Bike,
Strong Spoke Publishing, 2008

Acknowledgments

I want to thank the following people for helping me make this book a reality: poet Steven Schneider for hopping on a chairlift with me at Taos, talking to me, then introducing me to poet and publisher Mike Burwell. Cirque Press publishers Mike Burwell and Sandy Kleven for doing the things publishers do but mostly for inviting me into the Cirque community. Book designer Janna Christen for putting all the pieces together. Photographer Zigy Kaluzny who allowed me to use two of his images as models for drawings, the one of JT Brown walking down the boardwalk and the illustration of cork boots on the stairs to the cookhouse. Artist Dave Danioth for doing the cover and teaching me some things about drawing. Fellow civil engineer Lulu Pacheco for providing me a little bit of Spanish. Friends Bob and Mardel Honeywell for encouraging me when I needed it most. Singer, songwriter and brother of another mother, and father, Gordy Yancey who has been with me every step of the way. And my children Linton and Grace for sharing the love through thick and thin. I also want to thank Simpson Timber Company for hiring me several times, which allowed me to expend a lot of energy on the slopes of the Southern Olympic Mountains. Near the end of my logging career one of my coworkers told me I no longer had the eye of the tiger. That was a good thing. Uno mas, muchas gracias.

ABSOLUTELY NO CAULK SHOES

PROLOGUE

I owe the opportunity to edit and publish this story to a chance encounter I had with the author and narrator, Ed Knockle, in 2005. I was riding my mountain bike near Wynoochee Falls in the southern Olympic Mountains when I almost ran him over. Thirty years earlier we did collide at Grisdale, the defunct logging camp 10 miles down the road. This second time I was able to avoid him, and I would have continued riding, content to think that he looked similar to someone I had punched in the face a few times, had he not the courage to say, "Hey, aren't you Big Dave?"

"Fancy meeting you here, Ed," I replied after stopping and looking back. I had to bite my tongue to keep from calling him by his nickname. I doubt if it would have made him feel as good as I did upon hearing mine spoken and aimed at me for the first time in decades.

We talked for nearly an hour. He told me he was a fly fishing guide, owned and operated a fishing lodge in Patagonia, and was married to a beautiful Latina. That was hard to reconcile with the image of the man I had carried for so many years, but nobody at Grisdale knew him very well, and had it not been for the events he writes about in this book, nobody ever would have. Because I worked at Grisdale, I knew most of the characters involved in the story. After talking to many of my old friends who saw what happened, I developed a different slant on the story. But this is Ed's book and he didn't bring up the past while we were talking so neither did I.

He was very affable, and his interest in my life seemed genuine. I told him how I had quit logging about the time the spotted owl controversy heated up and that I started writing articles about the issue, how that had led me into sports and outdoor writing at which I still earned a regular paycheck from the *Tacoma News Tribune*. When I told him I had begun writing and publishing guidebooks on the side, and that I had my own little publishing company, for which I was the only author, he looked at me funny and told me he might send me something so I could diversify. I thought it was a joke. Like the two middle-aged businessmen that we were, Ed and I swapped business cards. We shook hands and went our separate ways. I didn't expect to see him again and chalked up this meeting to coincidence.

Five years later, out of the blue, I received a large brown envelope from Ed. When I opened it up I found a letter and a manuscript. I almost threw it away when I saw there was no self-addressed and stamped envelope, just kidding, but then I saw the DVD, so I read the letter. It explained that while camping on the Wynoochee he had been recounting to a digital voice recorder the story he witnessed and lived through at Grisdale. Back home in Argentina the recording had sat un-listened to for two years until his wife found the device, recharged the battery and turned it on. He told me he had been afraid that it would ruin their marriage if she heard it, but instead she encouraged him to type the words into a computer and fill in the blanks. They worked together on it for several years.

Having interviewed hundreds of sports stars, I know first hand how most people don't always talk in complete sentences, especially ones who have been bumped on the head a lot. Ed's narrative into the recorder was no different, but in the written version and subsequent re-writes, I think most of the bad grammar has been cleaned up. The other big difference between the recording and the book is that the dialogues are longer and more numerous in the written version. Plus the timing and details of some of the passages have also been changed to enhance their dramatic effect. I helped with that. The letter to me was essentially a query. He asked me if I'd read it and let him know if I thought it was publishable. While listening to the tale, then reading it, I realized I had been given a small segment of American folklore that needed to be preserved.

So here it is, folks. Believe it if you want to. Remember where it comes from. Back then, a man could trust only 10 percent of what another logger told him, unless he had seen it with his own eyes, and even then he would go along with a 50-percent distortion if it made for a better story. I know that publishing this book might ruin my reputation but imagine listening to it while sitting in a smoke filled bunkhouse on a night when the rain is pounding the roof and the heater is hissing as it cooks that day's precipitation and sweat out of the soggy wool socks, canvas rigging pants and hickory shirts hanging from the ceiling above it. There have been times I would have gladly gone back to that stinking place if I could, but those days are over. That life is over. Thank God I survived it. Not everyone did.

"Big Dave"
Tacoma, Washington
September 2012

1.

Day 1, recorded on the camp road while driving a rental car to Grisdale.

¡Hola mi linda esposa! I just skidded to a stop. That is easy to do on a gravel road, but they logged the land all the way to the mountains, as promised, and when I saw how naked it looks I hit the brakes. I can see Weatherwax from here. Weatherwax is the first mountain in the southwest corner of the Olympics, and Grisdale, the old logging camp, used to sit just inside its eastern flank. We couldn't see the high ground from this spot when I worked up there. We could only see the young trees along the sides of the road. In places their limbs reached the limbs of trees on the other side of the road and it was like driving through a tunnel. The trees were second growth meaning they replaced the old growth that originally stood here but the new forest was 35 miles thick and insulated us from the outside world. The green buffer made us feel safe as we logged the rest of the old growth on the mountains between camp and the Olympic National Park.

Thank you for giving me this digital recorder, Mamacita.

While flying up from Argentina, I listened over and over to the songs you and the girls sang. I like how you are teaching them the folk music you remember. It is beautiful and made me homesick before I got to North America, yet, because there is so much unused memory on the little machine, I assume you must have known I would find something to gripe about and need to talk.

I have started driving again. The recorder is sitting on my right thigh. I hope you can hear me over the noise. (The window is rolled down and on the recording you can hear the gravel beating the bottom of the rig. The radio is on, too, and tuned to an oldies station out of Seattle playing Led Zeppelin. I'm practically screaming above "The Stairway To Heaven.") As long as I keep my eyes on the road I know where I am but the moment I look at the fields of stumps I get lost. We used to drive this road by feel anyway. We knew where all the big potholes were and could read the bumps like braille. When rounding corners we sometimes hooked our inside tires in the ditch and hit the gas. On the straight stretches it was easy to go 60 and 70. That's how we drove when heading to town after a week or two in camp. Shagging back to camp after a weekend in town was a different story. Sometimes we were so hung over we could barely drive. I remember being so stoned I tried to look at every tree. Now I can hardly take my eyes off the rotten stumps of the original forest. They stick out above the second growth stubble like tombstones in a graveyard. Looking into the endless clear cut, the big rotten root wads that once held up the gigantic trees remind me of my friends. We logged old growth in the high ground as if there was no end. We should have sipped it like good whiskey. We guzzled that stuff, too.

I never wanted to come back here. I thought I made peace with the memories and buried the ghosts 20 years ago.

I wish I never had gotten that email from the detective in Grays Harbor County asking me to come up for an interview. That's when the memories started playing back in my mind.

DNA, the boon of modern criminology and the falsely accused. Apparently technology has advanced far enough to be able to process and identify samples of blood, skin, saliva, and semen taken from Ruby and the crime scene. Why can't they let her rest? I suppose living in Patagonia at the far end of the Western Hemisphere I could have made it difficult for the authorities, but my reluctance would have made it seem like I am guilty of something, and maybe I am.

(There is about a 5 minutes pause in the narration. Only road noise can be heard.)

Hey, the railroad is gone. I just got to where the road met the tracks from Shelton 35 miles to the east, but the rails and ties have been removed. (A second long pause...) There is Turnow Lake where they shot the mountain man. I don't know why they call it a lake. It always looked like a swamp to me. (And a third pause...) There are the big trees at the boundary to the National Forest. I'm glad they are still standing. The Forest Service left a string of them along the valley floor all the way to the National Park. They were a welcome sight when hauling ass back to camp. Our hootches were just up the road and even on the blackest rainy night when I was riding in someone's beater hoping it wasn't going to break down, I could feel those big bastards out there and knew I could stagger the last mile to camp on foot if I had to.

I just snaked through the S-turns near the garbage dump and am speeding down the last straight stretch at 70 again. To my right there's an empty field where the village once stood. I'm taking my foot off the gas, coasting the rest of the way up the slight incline and turning onto the access road. Shit, there is a big pile of dirt in the way.

(This time you can hear me skid to a stop.) The engine

is off. I am sitting at the roadblock with the windows down. I've been traveling non-stop for two days and our goodbye has subsided to a dull ache. The past and the present are trading places like water rolling down a stream. Minus the chatter of monkeys and the colorful birds, I am reminded of the Amazon. While I was in that jungle I realized how I had never appreciated this one. Now I am back. Now I can sit and listen to what these woods sound like. A raven cackled and glided ten feet above the ground down the road line leading into camp. All of a sudden I feel foolish for being here. Back then I was known as Knucklehead.

I AM KNUCKLEHEAD! (I screamed this out the window. Yelling felt good. On the recording I hear myself laugh then go silent for a moment.) Fucking-A, I was Knucklehead. I had them all fooled. Nobody knew who I was.

2.

Recorded Day 1 while sitting in my rental car at Grisdale.

Although I didn't come to camp as Knucklehead, I had been working on that identity a long time before I got here. I didn't graduate from high school until I was 19. I liked to get in trouble at the private schools where my mother sent me. Something about the rules pissed me off, not the written ones in every school, but the silent codes like how we were supposed to be smarter than kids from less fortunate families. Of course I was being raised by only one parent which was a stigma back then. My father had died before I was born and before my mother and he could get married. I don't think either one of them knew that my mother was pregnant until it was too late. My father didn't come from a rich family either. He had grown up on a dairy farm along the Chehalis River and had just gotten out of the Army after the Korean War. That was all I knew about him for a long time and it was enough to explain why I never got along with my cousins.

My mother never married or implied I was unwanted or a mistake. In fact she often told me I was a love child, which was embarrassing. She could have gone to an abortion clinic in Mexico and made it look like a vacation, but she didn't and I loved her for that. There were times when young though, that I wondered if my life was a good thing.

I started getting into fights in Junior High School and soon was stealing cars from tennis and golf clubs on Friday and Saturday nights. We always tried to return them before they were missed but eventually we got caught. My mom caved and sent me to military school. It was there or to juvenile home and at least I learned that I never wanted to be in the Army. I ran away to show them I could escape but there was no better option for me than to do my time. When I came home, private school was out of the question, so I enrolled at Garfield, a public high school. Everybody thought I was nuts because I was about the only white guy in there. My mom had gone to Garfield too in the late 40's back when there was more of a racial balance. For me it was another opportunity to be tough and get in fights but that didn't happen very often. I had something else going for me by then. I was a fast white guy and turned out for football.

My senior year I started at safety on what was almost an all black team. Not only that, I grew my hair long like a hippie. I loved it when guys called me a girl because it inspired me to kick their ass. I was the first to rumble after the games when we fought the players from the white teams in the alley next to the locker rooms at Memorial Stadium. If I started the fight it couldn't be labeled a racial confrontation. I think that was why the coach never kicked me off the team.

I was a good enough football player that some colleges were interested in me, but my grades were lousy so with nothing better to do I went to Olympic Junior College in Bremerton. They had a football team back then. Bremerton was also a Navy town. One day while buying gas a couple of jarheads at the neighboring pump whistled at me, and I discovered a new passion, fighting Marines.

It was a lot more interesting than fighting other football players or college kids. I can't say that the Marines fought any dirtier than I did. Many of them had spent time in Vietnam and knew how to fight to win. The gnarly ones with scars creeping out of their shirts and eyes still seeing death usually avoided me and assigned a fresh recruit to take me on. One night after a little scuffle in an alley, one old guy who looked like a sergeant was leaning against a wall watching. He told me he thought I'd make a good Marine and that I should think about joining. I guess that was a compliment. He even gave me a swig of his beer to wash the blood out of my mouth. I couldn't think of anything to say except "Maybe if there is ever a war worth fighting again." "See you there," he replied without smiling as he turned and walked back into the bar.

The truth is that I didn't win many of those fights. Usually nobody won. Somebody usually pulled us apart or yelled that the cops were coming. Plus I got my ass kicked more than once. But that didn't matter. By the end of my second season at Olympic, my grades still sucked. I enrolled for the next semester but sometime that winter quit going to class. Then one night a fight I got into turned ugly. They seemed to be getting worse. I don't know if it was because of the drugs and booze I was on but I blacked out while fighting a creep who made a pass at a woman I was talking to. I came to breathing hard with my friend Russ telling me I was getting spooky. He told me that I kept hitting the guy after he was on the ground and couldn't defend himself any more and if he hadn't been there to stop me I might have killed the sonofabitch.

A few weeks later I was at a party, talking to the same woman, and the same asshole came up behind me and broke a gallon jug of wine over my head. I fell onto a table and broke it apart. As I was standing up I grabbed a table leg and swung it at him. He raised an arm to protect himself. There was a loud snap and it wasn't the table leg that broke but the big bone in his forearm. He yelped like a dog and cradled his arm as he bent over. I couldn't help from hitting him in the head. I remember thinking that I could brain him and luckily I held back and tapped him just hard enough to knock him out.

The cops showed up instantly. They had been watching the place. After spending a couple of hours handcuffed at the hospital getting my scalp stitched up, I spent the next few nights in jail. If that jarhead hadn't hit me first, I probably would have spent a few months there. It also helped that my mom hired J.T. Brown, an up-and-coming attorney from Seattle, to defend me. That didn't stop the judge from telling me that I better straighten out or leave town. Well, I wasn't going to get any calmer. I knew that much. And while sitting in the courtroom it suddenly hit me that it was time to go to Grisdale. Consciously, I had never wanted to, but I think that every time I flushed the toilet and watched the turds swoosh down the toilet bowl I knew subconsciously that working at camp as a logger as my father had done was inevitable.

I need to get out of this rig. (You can hear the door opening as I get out. I grunt, sigh, and breathe heavily as I stretch, then you hear the sound of flowing water when I relieve myself. I fumble through my gear in the SUV, grab the recorder and slam the door. You hear a slap.) That was me killing a mosquito. (I open the car door again.) I better grab my hat. (The car door slams again and the recorder clicks off.)

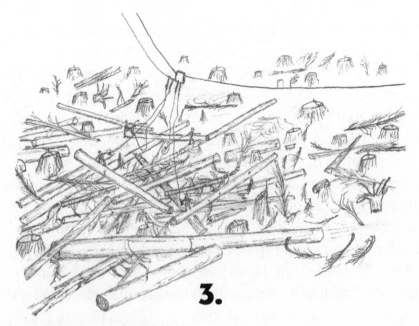

3.

Recorded Day 1, at Grisdale.

I'm sitting under a tree next to the spot where my old bunkhouse once stood. The tree used to be outside the window next to my bed, but the window is gone and the tree is a lot bigger.

Before I came in here, I walked to the yard as if looking for men to bullshit with while assembling for work. Hell, that place was so overgrown with new trees I could barely find it. Storm water had gouged out a streambed where the road through camp used to be and I had to wade through brush but I was able to confirm that the office, cookhouse, rigging shack, and every other building next to what used to be the big open space were gone. The location of the shops was the only easy place to find because the ground there was so polluted with grease and diesel that nothing was growing back.

I walked down to the village, too. The road there was less difficult to follow and the company hadn't planted new fir trees on that vacated clearing. Kid toys, auto parts, and broken furniture were scattered all over the place. It looked like a cyclone had carried away the little white houses and

9

picket fences. Never more than a visitor in the village, I stood at the edge a few seconds then hoofed it to where I am now.

Scrubby young alder and vine maple have plugged the holes where the bunkhouses sat and the straight path of the boardwalk can no longer be followed. A feint trail to the side leads in through the brush covering the old parking lot to what is now a stand of young Douglas firs. The company planted the trees in rows to replace a block of bunkhouses torn down in the early 60's after they finished the dirt road to town. Prior to that everyone had to ride the train to get to camp but a lot of men began commuting as soon as they could drive here. When I lived in camp, these trees were about twice as tall as a man and had limbs all the way to the ground. The camp girls, daughters of loggers who lived in the village, used to hangout in the patch of dog hair and spy on us. Now the trees are less easy to hide in. They are at least 50 feet tall and someone has cut off the dead lower branches so it is like a little park in here. There is an old fire circle too, so apparently I am not going to be the first person to spend the night here.

The buildings we lived in were long, narrow and built on skid logs so they could be hauled to the end of the tracks on a railroad car. A solid wall divided each one into two big rooms that had its own door to the boardwalk. The latrine was a short walk away but most of us peed into the weeds next to the stairs. It was an easy way to live. Bee rang the gut-hammer hanging on the cookhouse porch at 6 am, and we had to be at the yard by seven, no later. A bed maker who doubled as a narc made our beds. He was half blind and as long as you didn't leave any roaches in plain sight he didn't see them.

Some men liked living here so much they left wives and kids as far away as Seattle or Portland. They'd only go home Friday night and whenever we shut down for snow or heat. Some of them did that for decades, letting their wives raise their kids while they were away. They didn't hang out with us. You'd see them sitting in their bunkhouse reading or smoking a cigarette, watching.

I didn't want my mother or any one else in the family to know I was working in the family business until it was too late for her to do anything about it, so I didn't pull strings to get my job. It took me a month of calling the personnel office in Shelton every day before they hired me. I had to wait until the company called back all the crews after winter shutdown and they knew who was going to show up and who wasn't. Seeing how my mother was a daughter of a daughter of the man who had founded the company, I used her last name of Knockle, which was the one on my birth certificate and social security card, instead of my father's. I figured that since nobody named Knockle was a business executive in the company that the loggers wouldn't recognize it.

While in the company's Shelton office, my mind wandered as the woman in the personnel office gave me directions to camp. I already knew the way. When I was 16, I took my mom's Volvo one weekend while she was away and headed here. From Seattle I drove down I-5 to Olympia, turned west towards the ocean, hung a right at Montesano and drove up the Wynoochee River. The rain didn't let up for a moment after I entered Grays Harbor County. The pavement turned to dirt, and I thought I was lost, but I stayed on the main road like a gas station attendant in Montesano told me to until I finally saw the buildings. Then I turned off and drove through camp like a dumb ass tourist. What a dreary place. It was a Sunday and the place was dead. Who could live in this hole I remember wondering?

However, when I came up here to work on that spring night in 1975 and stepped onto the boardwalk the first time, I felt like I was coming home. The planks ran between two rows of two bunkhouses towards the latrine, the cookhouse and more bunkhouses. All the doors except for one were closed. Tattered canvas curtains or faded beach towels hung in most of the windows. One window had a macramé curtain and a light was actually on inside. Suddenly the door to that hootch burst open and a chubby hippie stepped out.

"Have you seen Snow?" he asked.

"No," I said.

"He's got some elephant weed, man. If you see him, tell him I'm looking for him, will you?"

"Okay."

He went back inside and closed the door, leaving me feeling as if I was in Alice In Wonderland. That guy had never seen me before and I didn't know who in the hell Snow was. The woman at the office had told me that I was supposed to sleep in bunkhouse 11. I saw that number in metal figures on the open door. Did someone leave it ajar for me? It was dark inside though. I walked up the three steps, entered the room, and flipped the light switch.

The first thing I noticed was the pea green paint that covered the plywood walls and ceiling. It reminded me of vomit. To the right of the door there was a bathroom sink stained with rust and what could have been the traces of real puke and blood. Above it the mirrored door of the medicine cabinet hung halfway open, slightly out of plum. It too was spattered with an assortment of crusty gobs. A gas heater built into the wall across from the door hissed pleasantly even though a couple of the windows were wide open. A haywired rack for drying clothes hung from the ceiling over the stove. A square wooden table and three miss-matched chairs filled in the middle of the room. I noticed a small hole in the floor and would soon learn that it was there for men to spit through while chewing tobacco. Mice used it too. Some old centerfolds hung on the walls. And most importantly, there was a metal bed in every corner, each covered with two mattresses, clean sheets under a canvas bedspread and a pillow with a crisp white case. There was also a wooden locker beside each crib, as well as a makeshift nightstand tacked to the wall and a reading lamp. After looking them over, I walked across to the bunk in the far right corner, looked out the window at the little trees, and set my laundry basket full of clothes on the floor next to the locker. My new cork boots were in a cardboard box on top, and I took them out and stood them on the floor. I sat on the mattress and bounced. The springs squeaked. What were the chances that my dad lived in this room, I wondered?

There was nothing to do but watch the daylight fade. After walking around a little and using the latrine, I returned to Bunkhouse 11, stripped down to my undershorts and got into the bed. It wasn't bad. I lay there half the night, I thought, listening to the heater kick on and off, too lazy to get out of bed and shut it down. The air breathing in from the woods felt good. (The recorder clicks off.)

I just walked out to my rental, a big SUV, to get a beer and brought back the entire cooler. Now I am sitting on it next to the tree, drinking a cold one. I wish I would have had a few of these on my first day of work.

I woke that morning to the clang of the gut hammer over at the cookhouse. It took a moment to realize where I was. Then I heard the springs of the bunk on the other side of the heater. I sat up and saw a guy on the edge of the bed in his underwear. "Who the fuck are you," I asked without thinking.

"Bob," he said, looking over at me and smiling slightly. "Bob Smith, and you?"

"Ed. Ed Knockle."

His little chuckle told me he had read my sarcasm. "Nice to meet you, Ed," he said as he stood up, turned his back to me, and reached into his locker for his clothes.

Shit. He was a big fucker, I remember thinking. A heavyweight. Bob wasn't real tall, right around six feet, but the back of his shoulders looked half as wide as that and they were covered with muscles. A cowboy hat sat on the table in the middle of the room. A pair of cowboy boots stood next to his bed. Had I been able to think of a cowboy joke at the moment, I wouldn't have told it.

"I didn't hear you come in."

"Some people call me Quiet Bob but you were snoring so loud I could have driven a motorcycle in here."

"I don't snore."

"How do you know?"

"No woman has ever complained about it."

"Have you spent the night with one, lately?"

"Just a couple weeks ago," I lied.

"Did you screw her in the morning?"

"I had to. It was either that or chew my arm off."

"You lucky fucker," he laughed. "How long have you been working here?"

"Today is my first day."

"Mine too."

"No shit. You have the same new work clothes as me." He had pulled his striped hickory shirt over his head, hooked his new suspenders onto the buttons of his pants, and was sitting on the edge of the bed still in his under shorts putting his socks on. My morning flagpole had shrunk to something less than half-mast, so I rolled out of bed and started getting ready, too.

"I hate to cut off the bottom of my pant legs," he said as he opened a pocket knife.

"They won't let us work if we don't."

When he was done sawing off the hem of his pant legs, he closed his knife and tossed it over to me.

14

"They send you to that old quack's house in Shelton for your physical?"

I remember every word of the ridiculous conversation. Lots of strange things happened that day. What could be more stupid than the desire to be a logger? I don't know what motivated Quiet Bob. He was a little fat around the middle and was probably slow. Me, on the other hand, I knew what I was doing. My father had died up here, and I wanted to know why.

When we entered the cookhouse, carrying our new cork boots, I was relieved to see almost everybody else was wearing the same outfit although the other men's rigging clothes were frayed and dirty while ours made it obvious we were green. In the chow line, the cook shoveled pancakes, eggs and sausage onto our plates then pointed to a table covered with more food, the spike table, and told us to go there and make lunches. Before we shuffled by, Dodge, the cook, looked up and told us that he hoped we would make it through the day and return for supper.

Next, we went to the office and met Turneau the accountant, or the logger's friend as some men called him. He was dressed in rigging clothes too, but his were only faded from being washed too many times, and not torn up from work. He had us stand at a long counter and fill out more paperwork while an older woman sitting at a desk inspected us over the top rim of her glasses. Turneau also sold us hard hats, gloves, and raingear from the company store. The money would be taken out of our first paycheck, if we lasted that long, he joked. Then he took us to meet Crank, the boss.

The man was sitting in a side alcove with his feet on a desk. Four or five other old men sat in chairs in front of him. These guys were a lot different than Turneau. All of them had on various versions of rigging clothes that hadn't seen much action but each one of them could have tied the accountant into knots if they wanted. Crank looked like he might do so for recreation even though it was obvious before he stood up that he was shorter than me. He was bald too, but tried to hide it with a flip-over plastered to his skull with hair tonic. However, his arms were as big around as Bob's.

"Here's your two new men from town, Crank," Turneau told him.

Crank looked us over. "Where you from?"

"Bremerton," I said.

"Iowa," Bob said.

"Farming?"

"I fed my share of hogs."

"Good. Farmers make good loggers."

"Do you know what crews they are going to?" Turneau asked.

"I got an idea," he said as he took his eyes off us and glared at Turneau.

"This way gentlemen." Turneau chuckled nervously and herded us out the back door. "Go up there and wait with everyone else." He nodded up past the back of the cookhouse to the throng of men standing in the yard, about 40 yards away. "You boys work safely. I drive the ambulance and don't want to have to take you to town."

"Crank seems like an asshole," I said when we were a few steps away.

"He probably has to be to run this place."

"You grow up on a pig farm?"

"Fuck, no."

We stood at the edge of the crowd. It wasn't raining so everybody was standing outside their crummies, what we called the crew busses, shooting the shit, but nobody talked to us. A big white school bus pulled into the yard and unloaded a bunch of men from town. Then another one came in and unloaded. A logging truck with an empty trailer stacked on back lumbered slowly past us. On the other side of the road a smaller group of men loaded chainsaws and gas cans into the beds of six packs, pickups with crew cabs. Those were the fallers. They looked more dignified than the guys on our side of the road. Beyond them, across the field covered by a loose formation of idling Kenworth and Peterbuilt trucks, clouds of black smoke belched into the air from a machine under a spar tree next to the railroad tracks. It was obvious that the contraption and the cat's cradle of cables above it lifted loads of logs off logging trucks and set them on railroad cars, hence its name, the reload.

Eventually the men in Crank's office drifted out. One of them went over to a crummy and talked to a bushy haired man in the passenger's seat of the cab. They both looked at us. The man from the office saw us watching, then aimed the horizontal peace sign in our direction and waved us over.

"My name's Hunt," he said when we got there. "I didn't get a chance to introduce myself in the office but I'm your siderod. Ott here is your hooktender. He's the boss of the crew I'm putting you on. When you're in the brush setting chokers though, you do what Snow tells you to do. He's your rigging slinger. He's in back, and I hear he's chucking his cookies out the window right now."

"He's not feeling too good today," Ott said, making a fake upside down smile of concern. "I don't know if that's a good thing or a bad thing for you. Did you guys watch that movie in the Shelton office?"

We nodded.

"Good. You know all about setting chokers then. Write your names down so I can put them on the timesheet, then get in back."

He handed me a clipboard and pencil. When I finished I handed it to Bob and stepped up through the side door.

The roof was high enough to stand under. A short aisle

between 2 rows of seats led to a long bench across the back. That's where I headed. I sat in the middle. The rest of the crew had taken all but one of the other seats, the one in the second row next to the man with his head out the window. That's where Bob sat. Ott had gotten out of the cab and looked in back.

"Everybody here?" Nobody answered him. "Great. Snow, you gonna be able to work today?"

"Yeah," he moaned.

"I got some tomato juice in my nose bag if that would help."

"Fuck you."

Even Bob and I laughed.

Ott slammed the door, crawled back up front, and the man driving the rig, named Jed, stepped on the gas and drove out of camp. The wind on Snow's face must have made him feel better because he pulled his head back in, sat down and turned to look at Bob and me.

"Who are you?" he asked.

"Your new fucking," someone answered for us.

"That might not be a good idea today. I might puke on them and they probably wouldn't like that."

What could we say? His voice was deep and respectful.

"I did puke on a gal once while fucking her." He smiled and turned away from us as he closed his eyes. "If you last, I'll tell you about it someday."

We rode in silence for a while. The crummy was in a loose caravan driving up the 300 road along Lake Wynoochee, which was a reservoir behind a small dam. Eventually we turned onto a spur road and began climbing the ridge to the east. Snow opened his eyes again and looked at us.

"You better get your boots on." His were already laced up. "When we get to the landing you're not gonna have time to crack your ass and shit until noon, if you make it that long."

18

He turned back around and shut his eyes again.

We drove past stands of big trees, little trees, and no trees. The crummy turned onto a steeper road that angled across fields of stumps and slash that appeared to be nearly vertical. The guy sitting next to me lit up a cigarette and I almost gagged.

The road finally leveled out on top of a ridge. That triggered the other men to close their lunch buckets and screw the cups back onto their steel thermoses. Snow re-opened his eyes. "Anybody got some snoose they can share?" he asked. A man reached out with a can of Copenhagen. When Snow stretched his arm out for it, I noticed a tattoo on his forearm that made me shudder. After shoveling a huge amount behind his lower lip, he handed it back, which allowed me to get another look at his arm.

The tattoo was of a long bloody dagger wrapped in banners of Latin words. One phrase stuck out. "Semper Fi. U.S.M.C." He was a Marine. Shit, I swore to myself.

He looked at Quiet Bob and me again and shook his head. "Two green men. Someone must have told Crank I was sick and hungover. He'll be laughing about it all day and disappointed if I don't fire one of you."

"That's motivational," I couldn't help but quip.

"You better be motivated."

I kept my mouth closed and glared at the back of Quiet Bob's head wondering what he was thinking.

We passed a logging truck sitting at a wide spot. The truck driver acknowledged our passage by lifting his eyes from the book he was reading. Jed turned the crummy around in another wide spot then backed up the road. The crummy stopped. We stepped out the door onto the landing. Snow told us to put our lunches in one gunny sack and our raingear in another. "I hope you packed some good sandwiches because I didn't make a lunch. One of you probably won't make it to noon and I bet my appetite will be back by then." He climbed into the crummy to get something he forgot. Ott had gotten out of the cab and came over to us. He was still in his slippers.

"You two do what Snow tells you to do and you'll live to see the end of the day. He may send your asses down the road but at least you'll be able to tell your grandchildren how you were a logger for part of a day. He's not happy to have to break in two green men at once but if he hadn't shit canned 2 guys last week, he wouldn't have that problem now."

I was tired of being warned how tough it was going to be. The wind was more interesting. The air felt ten degrees cooler than in camp. Industrial and human trash littered the oil stained crushed rock under my feet. Only the stacks of logs fanning out from the machine with a huge grapple made any sense. That and the steel tower at the end of the yarder. It had to be over 100 feet tall and it was definitely the focal point of the logging show. Cables radiated from the top of it like a spider web. Some were meant to hold it up and others there to pull logs.

Snow climbed back out of the crummy wearing a belt with a square metal tube riveted to it. He was carrying another one. About that time Jed, who was also the yarder engineer, pushed the ignition button and the machine rumbled to life. The smoke puffing out of the vertical exhaust pipe quickly changed from black to grey to white. Jed gunned the machine a couple of times. He was standing in the window of the cab ten feet up smiling at us. He'd sit up there all day watching the cable drums, which were at least six feet in diameter. There were three of them and each held thousands of feet of tightly wound line. With switches, levers and pedals he commanded each to wind cable in or slack it off. Jed was in his late thirties or early forties, nearly twice as old as me, and combed his dark hair back like the actor Robert Mitchum.

"The sonofabitch doesn't even look hungover," Snow

said.

We turned our attention back to him.

"You take this," he said as he handed the extra device to Bob. "Strap it around your waist like mine. It's the backup whistle in case mine runs out of juice or I get snuffed. They work like this. Turn it up on end then clamp down on the handle." When he did so, a whistle as loud as one on a train blared from a loud speaker on top of the yarder's cab. Both Bob and I jumped which amused everyone. "One whistle stops the rigging. Blow seven longs if I become incapacitated."

Jed pulled a bottle of aspirin out of his shirt pocket and held it out as if offering some to Snow. Snow gave him the finger. I was the only one who didn't laugh. I didn't need to be told that Bob had just been promoted. With two pink scars zigzagging across my pale shaved scalp, I looked like a crazy man and could understand why Snow hadn't given the whistle to me. I also had given Snow some lip. But they already were fucking me a voice inside my head bitched, and I didn't have time to pout.

"Now let's go get dirty," Snow said then turned around and ran back past the crummy and loader.

"You better get your asses in gear," Ott said not too kindly. We sprinted to catch Snow but that would prove to be impossible. As soon as he had gotten past the cold deck of logs he turned towards the downhill side of the road and disappeared. By the time we got to the edge, he was at the bottom of a slope of road fill, thirty yards away, looking up for us. "Hurry!" he barked then turned again and began loping in big strides down the logged off mountainside. The huge clearcut angled steeply about a thousand vertical feet to the bottom. One of the cables hung from the top of the tower across the valley to a tailhold stump in a field of baby trees at least a mile away. Almost all the logs on our side of the cable had been removed and thousands were still left waiting for us on the other side. Bob and I bailed off and skidded down through the gravel into the hole.

The brush was a no man's land. The ground looked like artillery had worked it over. Troughs of bare earth gouged into the ground by moving logs provided short corridors of easy running then ended in piles of limbs and tree tops that blocked our way like barbed wire. We had to jump or climb over rotten and shattered logs when there was no quicker way around, and I found out I had cut the bottom of my pant legs off too short when sticks and brush began scrapping, gouging and tearing the bare skin exposed above my boots. Every once in a while Snow turned around and yelled "Hurry!" I listened to Bob behind me hoping he was having a more difficult time than I was. I wanted to see him quit or get fired.

Snow was headed for the logs that jutted to our side of the cable. When he got there, he blew in some whistles. The skyline lowered down slowly, sat on the ground a moment off to our left a hundred feet or so, then tightened back up and rose into the air. I heard something rolling down the skyline. I looked up and saw the carriage. It was made of two big plates of steel that sandwiched and hung from the skyline on rollers. The front of the carriage was shackled to another cable, the mainline, that Jed was paying out from the yarder. Two 40-foot-long chokers hung from the bottom of the carriage and another one hung from the hardware connecting the carriage and the mainline. The choker bells, the casted steel fasteners at the end of the chokers, clanged merrily as the rigging passed us by. Snow was standing on a log that ran across the hill under the cable.

"You better get here before the chokers do!" he yelled.

More whistles blew and the big cable slacked towards the ground. Snow walked down the log to where the cables were going to land. I jumped onto the log as he blew another whistle to stop the rigging when the choker bells were waist high. I thought that my momentum was going to carry me off the other side but the nails on the bottom of my boots grabbed the log like claws and I stopped on a dime. I started walking down the log towards the slinger, catching my breath and listening for Bob. He landed three seconds after I did, not long enough.

The chokers had braided themselves and Snow ignored us as he untangled them. "I better not always be the one doing this," he said abstractly. When he was done, he swung us each a snare. Bob got the one in front, which by the way meant towards the yarder and was the choker reserved for the bull choke. I got the one in the middle, and Snow took the one in back.

"The way it works out here is that I tell you what logs to choke." I didn't listen closely to his instructions. It seemed simple. "Let me know if you need more slack." "We work as a team." "The name of the game is to get the wood to the landing as fast as possible, and I don't give a fuck about making it easy for the welfare bitches on the landing." I liked that one. "Pull hard and it comes easy."

Getting my choker around that first log didn't seem like it was going to be difficult but after I stuck the choker through a hole under the log and climbed over to the other side I discovered the choker had pulled itself out of the hole. Luckily, Snow appeared over there right then and shoved it to me.

"Sometimes I feel more like a kindergarten teacher out here," he griped.

By the time I figured how to stick the babbit at the end of the choker into the hole on the choker bell, creating a noose, and climbed back on top of the log, Bob and Snow were standing in the clear.

"Run or die," Snow shouted. I took off down the log towards them. "The whistles are in!" I heard them blow and as I jumped off the end I heard the yarder roar and sensed the cables move. I landed next to Snow and turned in time to see the cables pull into the wood.

There was a pause as the chokers tightened and held the carriage down. The engine on the yarder slowed a notch as it built tension in the skyline and main line. Bob and I had choked two logs 40-foot long and big enough around to put on the bottom of a load. Those were bunk logs. Snow had choked what looked like a pile of brush and it began to move as if a big animal was trying to escape from beneath it. Limbs and sticks snapped. Bob and my logs rolled and jumped uphill. Then the whole pile lifted in the air. Snow's choker contained three or four smaller logs that stuck out in different directions but he had choked them in a way that the pecker poles began to swing neatly beside one another. A shower of debris fell off as all the logs thunked together. The skyline pulled the turn into the air as if it didn't weigh anything. That was cool. Snow blew in three more whistles and Jed began winding faster on the mainline. Watching the cables lift the turn into the air and pull it up the hillside was powerful stuff, something I never grew tired of. I think most tree huggers would have found it fascinating too.

Right before the logs reached the top, we heard the inch and a half thick skyline knife to the ground. Sticks flew into the air when it hit. Smoke rose from a log it sawed over for a moment. Snow told us that the engineer had to dump the skyline in order to land the logs. Sure enough we saw the butt of the logs disappear over the edge of the landing.

The sound of metal striking metal echoed across the valley. Snow walked out to the cable, which lay harmlessly on the ground now. "Stay there," he said when we started to follow. "Take a breather. You're going to need it." We watched him peer under a pile of brush. He didn't have much time. The cable began moving uphill and he walked back towards us.

"There are two types of crews," he said while looking at us and ignoring the skyline lifting into the air behind him. "Those that fuck the dog and those that highball. Now we start highballing."

4.

Day 1, back under the tree next to where my old bunkhouse stood.

Mama went ballistic when I called and told her that I was working at Grisdale.

You can't do that to me! You'll be killed like your father. I won't let it happen. That was the gist of what she said among the tears and curses.

"You can't do anything about it," I replied. "We're a union outfit. I'm a member now. Uncle Pete can't snap his fingers and have me fired." That was stretching the truth because I was at the beginning of the probationary period when they could fire me without much trouble, but my lie did the trick.

"You are right," she admitted. "You'd resent me the rest of your life."

On the other end of the phone line in the red phone booth outside the worn out recreational building, I reflected a moment on the fact that I loved my mother. "I'm not doing this to hurt you."

"I know."

"It feels like it is something I need to do. I want to make

it up here without any help from the family. These guys don't know who I am and I'd appreciate it if nobody told them."

"I'll try to keep that from happening. My cousins will actually be happy you are working for them."

"That's not why I did it. I don't give a . . ."

"Everyone loves you."

"Yeah right. They love their dogs, too."

"Do you need anything?"

"Come on mom, you know that's a silly question. I have everything I need right here. A job. Three squares a day. And a boss who is trying to fire me. What more could a guy want?"

"It doesn't sound fun. Is the food still as good as it used to be?"

"I don't know what it used to be like. Dodge, the cook, is no chef but there are plenty of steaks and he makes good pies. I'll probably gain 20 pounds."

"Promise me one thing."

"What's that?"

"Don't climb any trees."

"Is that how my dad was killed?"

"Yes."

"You never told me that."

"I know. I shouldn't have said anything about it now, either."

"Why not?"

She didn't answer me but that little bit of information was huge. My father was killed climbing a tree. What did it mean? In the short time I had worked there I had already caught on that climbers were all stars but I had not yet seen a man in a tree and had no real picture of it in my brain. How did somebody die doing it? Falling out of a tree, obviously, but what would cause that to happen? I had much to learn. Staying alive while setting chokers was enough for now.

As I lean back against the tree now and watch the flames in my campfire, I try to remember what I did know about my father back then. Not much.

Mama only made sure to tell me over and over again that she loved my father. She told me that she was sad that he hadn't lived to meet me and be my father. She told me that in order to not feel bitter she had to let go of his death and accept how lucky she was to have had a child fathered by someone she loved so much. That part I believed because she never seemed bitter to me. I'm the one who was angry. I figured she didn't tell me much else about him so I wouldn't follow his footsteps. That sure in hell didn't work.

Here is what I knew at the time when I started working at Grisdale. Her family, the family that owned the timber company, had a lodge on Lake Nahwatzel between camp and the town of Shelton. Various branches of the family spent part of each summer at the lodge, oftentimes overlapping their visits so they could have reunions. My mother quit going to the lodge when she was a teenager, but after her first year in college, she and some of her cousins decided to meet up and do it again for old times' sake.

One of the traditions was to ride the train to Grisdale and have dinner in the cookhouse. I'm sure they stirred up the young bucks when they walked in. My father was in there at the time and he and my mom made eye contact. She told me he didn't make an idiot out of himself like some of the others.

That next weekend there was a big dance at the Nahwatzel Grange. That was a yearly event that was still going on when I worked at camp. My mother and her cousins went. So did my father. He asked her to dance. She told me he could jitterbug and foxtrot a lot better than the other loggers. They fell in love and saw each other on the weekends. She didn't figure out she had gotten pregnant for a month or two. He died in the fall of 1953 before she had a chance to tell him.

The revelation that he died while climbing confirmed my belief she knew a lot more than she wanted to tell me. I knew I couldn't pry it out of her. I had been trying to do that since I was a little kid. I was going to have to wait. Something told me that pieces of the story were going to fall out one chunk at a time. I don't know where that bit of wisdom came from. I saw myself as being angry, self-destructive and stupid.

My mother had also been a hellion if that was any consolation. I wasn't something new for the family to deal with. She told me that for as long as she could remember her awareness of having more than most people made her feel awkward. Her parents lived in Broadmoor, which was a gated community of moneyed families, mansions and a golf course in the middle of Seattle. To get to downtown for shopping or business, people in Broadmoor, and in neighboring Madison Park where other family members lived, had to drive through the deteriorating central district. Black people lived there. They were replacing the Italians. Whenever her parents drove through those neighborhoods, they told the children to lock the doors and roll up the windows. They didn't want the boogieman stealing their little girls and boys. It had the intended effect on my mom when she was a little girl but it set her up for the boogie-woogie man later on. Long before she became a teenager, she figured out why the people staring at them didn't smile. Their eyes were hungry, envious and pissed off. The black people who came into their houses to clean smiled and laughed with their mouths but their eyes held a different story. She told me she saw walls everywhere.

When she was a teenager, she started climbing over them. Like me she was kicked out of the exclusive schools her parents sent her to. Back in the late forties and early fifties it didn't take much. Smoking cigarettes in the girls can, wearing the wrong clothes, swearing at teachers and reading books by communists got her in trouble but her biggest offense was being unrepentant. They couldn't break her. She skipped school. When her parents restricted her, she went over the wall.

They finally relented and allowed her to go to public high school. She went to Garfield, the same one I went to. Among a student body that was growing darker every year, she settled down enough to do her homework. When she graduated, she chose to go to the University of Washington rather than to an Ivy League school in the east. The U of W was acceptable to the social elite as long as their kids joined the right sororities and fraternities but that wasn't going to happen with Mama. She got a room in a girl's dorm. The university stimulated her. Ideas were generating in schools across the country that would help nourish the Civil Rights Movement. The Cultural Revolution was about to ignite. Socializing with everyday people was a lot of fun, too.

Much of that came to an end when she became pregnant with me. She was only 20 years old. I spent a lot of my early life feeling sorry for myself. I fantasized about what my father was like and how being raised by him would make me happy. My mother did the best she could and that turned out to be great. Faced with the reality of having to raise a kid, she let up on the battle against her parents. It took a while though. She actually gave birth to me while living in a home for unwed mothers. Soon after that she moved into a house on top of Capital Hill. A friend she made at the home for unwed mothers, and her new baby, moved in with us. I can vaguely remember Carl. We were like brothers until his mom met some guy and moved to California with him when I was four. Mama also hired an old Mexican lady to live with us. Nina Sanchez. She, her husband, and grown children were migrant workers but then her husband was killed in a car accident in Yakima. Not long after that Nina came to Seattle to work in a fish cannery but she didn't get along with the Asians working there so she answered my mom's ad for help.

Mama welcomed Nina's family into our home when they were in town, which was often. That is how my love of all things Spanish was born. Nina had a temper, which probably helped foster the one in me.

Mama became a beatnik, then a hippie. In the eighties she got into New Age. But when I was little, she also went back to school, took classes in psychology and eventually earned a master's degree. After working in a clinic for a while, she started her own therapy practice, which was groundbreaking in Seattle at the time. I traveled all over the world with her too. She and her sisters acquired a place in Puerto Vallarta that they shared, and I spent a lot of time down there back when it was just a fishing village. I met rock stars, movie actors, artists of every kind, politicians, gangsters, and enough anonymous rich people to never have to look hard for a job again. We were part of the jet set, but it was my mother's work that sustained her. She had no interest in the price of timber but would mull over her clients' problems for weeks. I'd catch her on the phone all hours of the night talking to other psychologists, psychiatrists, spiritual counselors, gurus, or anybody else she thought who could help her heal someone's psychic wound. When mine burst out, she couldn't do anything about it. I sure wasn't going to talk to anybody she sent me to. Her instinct was to mother and protect me from the hurts of the world. Me going to work at Grisdale reopened the wound in her. It nearly did her in. While I was becoming a rigging man, she developed an addiction for an experimental anti-depressant and was faced with a crisis that pointed her down the path towards healing. Those are her words. I felt bad about that but everybody must leave his or her mother, and I had to close my heart as I listened to her cry on the other end of the phone when I told her I had become a logger.

It's dark now and I'm lying in my sleeping bag next to the fire I built in the pit that was here. The ground is hard but at the moment I am comfortable. I cooked a can of beans and roasted some hot dogs for dinner. I have a carton of milk and some cereal, a loaf of bread and a jar of peanut butter, two beers shy of two six packs of Budweiser, coffee, a jug of orange juice, an assortment of energy bars, paper plates and bowls, a coffee mug, and a pan to boil water in. The light from my fire is dancing with the darkness on the tree trunks. I hope I don't see any ghosts. I don't need to talk to any of them again. I am tired. I am grateful this spot feels familiar and that I don't need four walls around me and a locked door or loaded gun to feel safe. I miss my wife and children who are half a world away and beyond cell phone range. My appointment at the Sheriff's office is four days from now. I am going to sleep.

5.

Day 2, starting in morning at camp.

I used to hate hearing these birds when I woke up. Back then I could have stomped every one of them. Now I could lie here all morning listening to their songs. Can you hear them? (The sounds of birds chirping.) I don't know if they are sparrows, swallows or what. That's embarrassing.

I'm out of the sack now, sitting on my cooler drinking a cup of camper's coffee. Sunlight is hitting the treetops to the west and soon it will reach the bottom of the valley. The weather is going to be good today. September is usually nice up here. My sleeping bag is rolled up. I've put my camping gear back in the shopping bag and the food in the cooler. The fire has just about burned out. When I'm done with my coffee, I'm going to carry all this stuff back to the rig and try to drive to the first logging show I worked on.

Now I'm driving. At first glance the land hasn't changed much. The jagged ridgeline to the west across the lake is as good to see as the face of an old friend. Since I have been away, the brown clearcuts on the mountain slopes have turned green.

Due to the age and density of trees, each cut is a different shade than the one next to it. Another difference is that the valley feels empty. At most there are only a handful of people within a hundred square miles of here, if any besides me. Thirty years ago there would have been ten yarders within the drainage. Whistles would have been blowing and engines roaring as the big machines dragged logs up and down the hills. Twenty-five trucks would have been rumbling along these roads hauling wood to the transfer. Dozens of chainsaws would have been playing mournful songs while the men holding them fingered the throttles and the teeth chewed through growth rings. Rants of an angry rigging man would drift down a valley. An old man named Sprint called it singing. These hills were full of music back then. Now they are silent. Now I can feel the void left behind as I drive slow with the windows down.

Near the end of the lake I hang a right onto the spur we took my first day logging. The road is still intact. It winds up through stands of new trees that cover slopes I remember as being bare. Yesterday it was the lack of trees that made me feel lost.

I'm almost at the top of the ridge now and can see that the next road I have to turn onto is covered with dirt, rocks and stumps that have slid onto the grade from the hillside above it. In some spots the road has sloughed away. I'm going to have to walk the last mile.

It's a nice hike. Being on foot gives me a closer look at how the road is blending into the land and a new forest is growing back. I'm glad I brought plenty of water. There isn't any water up here this time of year. The view of Lake Wynoochee can drive a man crazy some days.

I just made it to the landing. I can see where the yarder stood. The pile of slash around the edge of the landing was burned and the remains have rotted away. The bowl below me is full of new trees that are four or five times my height.

They thin out as they get closer to the landing and I can see over the top of them. In some places the new forest is thin enough that traces of skid roads are still visible radiating down from the landing.

Hey, there is a big stump I remember. It's not far off the landing, so what the hell, I think I'll stumble down and sit on it again.

My legs are hanging over the rotten downhill side of the stump that logs bashed into. The bark has fallen off the rest of it but I bet the wood deep down is solid and it would make a good tailhold. The tree that stood here must have been a nice stick. By the time I showed up, the crew had already logged past here. The only reason I remember it is because I got to take a good rest here that first day. Snow was relentless. He kept yelling at us to hurry. In for our jobs and out for our lives. Today. Run or die. The brush was a bitch. It grabbed, poked and tripped us as we ran. It tore our clothes and whipped us raw.

Snow knew where to step without looking. "Don't think about where to put your feet," he suggested during a more friendly moment. "Yeah, right," Bob mumbled. He sank into the brush like a water buffalo in mud. I was more like an angry pit bull. Everything about the brush pissed me off and I wanted to make it obvious to Snow that he should send Bob down the road. I beat him to the chokers every time Snow spotted the rigging. I tried to set my choker faster than he did but, like I said, the brush could make me lose my mind. I pulled and pounded on the debris blocking my choker with no regard for myself. I swore at it, loudly. Snow and Bob must have thought I was nuts. I hated it when Bob showed up on the other side of a log from me, pulled out a stick or two, then stuck his hand underneath and said "shove it through, Ed." However, that only happened a couple of times. After a couple of hours, he began to get that look I had seen on the faces of lots of big men during football practice at the start of the season. Maybe he was going to quit. That would be nice. But to tell you the truth I almost did late in the morning after we heard a truck chugging up the road on the other side of the valley.

"There's Sprint," Snow said.

"Who's he?" I asked.

"He drives the line truck."

"What's that?"

"The front half of an old logging truck with a big cable drum on the back. He's going to help Ott change roads.

'What's changing roads?"

"Where we swing the skyline over more logs after we're done with this one. You guys get a break. All you have to do is hump up to that stump on the knob while I hang back and help them."

When he said that, Bob and I looked up the hill and saw the stump I am sitting on now. It looked like it was on top of Mt. Rainier to me and probably like Everest to him. After logging the last turn on that road, Snow let us drink out of the stream one last time then sent us up the hill. He didn't have to tell us we better not let him beat us up there, either.

I wanted to smoke Bob's ass so climbed as hard as I could. A little ways up the hill I turned to look back and saw him only 10 yards behind me, so I climbed harder. While doing so, all sorts of things were going on that didn't make sense. The rigging went by us then came back up the hill dragging a long skinny cable. Sprint and Ott screamed at each other. When I looked back again, Bob was maybe twelve yards behind me. As my breathing became more difficult and my legs grew tired, I heard someone pounding on metal back at the tailhold. The skyline came loose and slithered downhill. Jed began pulling on it but the cable didn't rise into the air. Whistles blew. Snow yelled "GO AHEAD ON HER, SPRINT!"

36

"GOIN A–HEAD ON 'ER," Sprint yelled back, then fired up the pony engine on the back of the line truck. It didn't have much of a muffler but I could hear brush snapping and old rotten logs getting pushed out of the way as the old man pulled the end of the skyline to the new tailhold stump with a long cable from his machine.

I looked back again and saw Bob had inched closer to me and Snow was now climbing faster than both of us. That's when I realized I wasn't doing much better than my bunkmate. We had covered three–quarters of the distance to the stump but the hill was getting steeper and we were slowing down. My legs felt as if they might cramp up any time. That was when I realized Snow was right. We were on the same rigging crew and had to work as a team for it was possible that neither one of us would make it to the end of the day. We needed one another.

I might have slowed down. I knew a faster runner could encourage a slower one by staying slightly out of reach rather than by running away. Then Ott and Sprint commenced yelling again which provided some weird comic relief. Apparently there was a problem over there and we weren't so green that we didn't know a delay was going to be good for us.

"We beat him," I said when I sat down on this stump the first time. Bob was only a few steps behind me. He sat down in the dirt and looked across the valley without saying anything. The sweat was pouring down his face so hard I swear the top of his hard hat looked wet. Snow took his last step up the hill and stared at us a moment as he caught his breath, then turned and looked across the canyon too. Ott finally blew the whistle, three deuces, to cable up hard and pull the dogleg out of the skyline. All eyes were on the skyline as Jed began pulling in the slack. Something held it down at first and feeling the tension in the cable start to build I slid off the top of the stump to the side Snow and Bob were on.

A second later the cable got tight enough to bust through whatever was holding it down. It sprung into the air like a bowstring and threw a rotten log and an old stump into the air. Dirt and rocks fell away like the tail of a comet. Jed kept reeling in line as fast he could. The cable didn't quite land when it fell and swung towards the new tailhold a few feet off the ground mowing down three acres of baby trees.

The wave in the line traveled up to the tower. The butt rigging pounded the side plates of the carriage and the tower tested all eight guylines as it shook but Jed kept pulling until Ott blew one whistle to stop. The big cable swooshed sideways up high a few times then swayed to a stop over a new road of logs for us to choke and yard.

"SHE'S ALL YOURS, SNOW," Ott yelled across the valley.

"O-K," he yelled back then signaled for the yarder engineer to ship us the chokers. "Road changes are usually dramatic on this crew," he said to us.

Before the rigging came back though Buffy, the chaser, stuck his head over the landing. The machines were off and he was so close he didn't have to yell. "It's lunchtime, Snow. Are you guys going to eat on the landing?"

Snow looked at us. "No, you better send the nosebag down."

"Enjoy your picnic," Snow said after we grabbed the gunny sack off the rigging and sent in the turn. "I'm gonna go leave a shit in that dog hair and then walk to the landing to see if I can bum some food."

I watched him stride across the slope and disappear behind some little trees that had escaped the destruction. Bob ate half a sandwich and drank a carton of juice before falling asleep. My body was aching but I just sat here in a stupor until Snow came back a half hour later. "Find any food up there?"

"Not much and I'm hungry."

I suspect Snow smoked some of that elephant weed when he crapped. "He said we could eat his food." I pointed at Bob with my eyes.

"Go ahead," Bob grunted from the ground.

"You from around here?" Snow asked me after grabbing the other sandwich out of Bob's lunch sack.

"No. Bremerton."

"I knew a couple of guys who got stationed there after Nam. How'd you wind up here?"

"A judge told me to leave town. I got in too many fights with a Marine."

"Is he the one who left his mark on your head? It kinda looks like the Marine Insignia."

"Great. I hope he's still in a cast. I broke his arm."

That amused Snow. A moment later some whistles blew, our slinger repeated them, and the skyline, which had been lying on the ground, slithered up the hill then lifted into the air. Bob opened his eyes and stood up. Here came the chokers.

The rests between turns weren't long enough. After every turn, I sat down alongside my bunkmate and tried to gather enough energy to set another choker. Every time I looked up, the chokers were screaming down the skyline towards us. What an idiot I was for coming up here. God knows what Bob was thinking about.

"Do you think we are going to have to hike back up to the landing at the end of the day?" Bob asked me quietly while Snow was picking out the next turn.

Snow heard him though. "The crummy can't drive down here and pick us up," he laughed.

Bob didn't say anything. Neither did I. We were a long ways away from the landing by then and thinking about humping up the hill again was too much to bear. To make it worse, Snow began pulling out his pocket watch after every turn. "How much fucking time is left?" I snapped.

"Maybe 30 minutes."

"What time do we quit?" I asked. I really wanted to cry.

"Some days Jed blows slack off at three-forty. Some days at three-fifty. It depends on if we need a few more logs to finish off a load. But don't worry. We never work past four unless we're working OT and nobody has said anything about that today."

Three forty came and went. Two turns later, while reeling in the logs, Jed blew a shave-and-a-hair-cut, the signal that the day was done.

Bob and I looked at Snow waiting to follow him up the hill. Instead, he turned and began running down hill.

"Where you going?" Bob yelled.

He stopped and looked back. "Out to the road. The crummy picks us up about a half mile from here. It's all downhill. You better hurry. Nobody likes to wait very long." With that he turned and took off.

"What an asshole." Bob muttered.

We followed him as best we could along the bottom of the valley until we rounded a corner and saw the crummy sitting atop a bank of road fill covering a culvert. Jed had his window down and was smoking a cigarette. "There they are," we heard him say. Snow stuck his head out his window in back and yelled "Today," one more time. The men in back with him laughed. I remember slowing down so that Bob and I climbed the bank and got into the crummy together. I remember thinking how none of the pricks who had worked on the landing all day better give me any shit.

We sat down in our seats.

"How many logs we get?" Snow asked nobody in particular.

"A hundred and thirty seven," Buffy told him.

"That sucks."

"Considering you had two green men and were only flying three chokers, that's not so bad."

"And you were puking your guts out this morning," the older guy in back added. That got a laugh.

"Slacker One has been breaking two hundred every day for the past month and I'm tired of hearing about it from Big Dave at night. We should be kicking their ass on this show."

"We don't get paid for how many logs we get," the older guy replied.

"You don't fool me," Snow smiled at him. "You love it. Getting lots of wood gives you a hard on just like it does the rest of us."

"The only hard on I get is when I'm socking the wood to the old lady."

"Buffy claims he's afraid to bend over when he sees you out of the loader."

I wasn't paying much attention to the bullshit about packing fudge. I was thinking how somebody kept score and wondering who Big Dave was. Slacker One was obviously another yarder. That we had to kick their ass made sense. I realized that logging was a sport and Tower Seven was a team.

After taking a shower, Bob lay down on his bunk and went out like a light. I was starving and walked up to the cookhouse. Snow was there sitting with a bunch of guys and I ignored him. Being Tuesday it was seafood night. Prawns the size of ping-pong paddles and chunks of deep fried halibut as big as choker bells. I ate two plates of them, a plate of French fries, and two bowls of ice cream.

"Where's your partner," Snow asked when I got up to leave.

"He's asleep."

"What you do to him, Snow?" The guy asking him the

question had to be Big Dave. He was bigger than Bob, with a full beard and slabs of muscle across his chest and shoulders that could only have been cultivated by lots of time in a weight room pumping the big bar and plates. He looked at me like I was dirt too, and I wondered what Snow was doing eating with him.

"I hope he shows up tomorrow," Snow said.

"He will," I boasted, also hoping I was right. I knew I wouldn't feel like getting out of bed and if he balked I might too.

We made it to the yard in the morning. The second day was worse than the first and the day after that was more painful. Bruises, welts and knots collected on my body faster than mosquito bites and the way Bob wallowed through the brush at times I knew it was no fun for him. He was as stupid and stubborn as I was. We grumbled to each other during the day but at night he went to bed right after dinner. It was a lonely period. I say that as a joke but it's true. I didn't talk to any of the other men in camp.

Screw it. I'm tired of sitting on this stump. I'm going to walk down to the bottom of the hole.

Somehow we increased our log count each day. On Wednesday the second week we cracked 200 logs and ten loads. By then Bob was beating me in and out of the turns once in a while. On Thursday, Snow appeared on the other side of a log I was choking and asked, "Do you eat your fucking or fuck your eating?"

I had to think about that a moment.

"I know. I've been trying to figure that out for a long time," Snow said.

By then, Bob had showed up assuming we needed help. Snow asked him the same question.

"Depends on how drunk I am."

That led to a philosophical discussion that lasted the rest of the day, which was a first, and on the crummy ride back to camp, Buffy asked Snow if he was going to stump break us any time soon. He said he wanted to watch. Snow called him a pervert. "Next you'll want to watch me jerk off," he said and everybody but Bob and me laughed. "Don't worry," Buffy reassured us. "I've never met a man who didn't enjoy getting stump broke, especially by Snow."

Friday, right before noon, when I finished setting my choker I looked up and saw Snow pulling hard on a choker that Bob was trying to get around a log. He needed a couple more feet of cable to bell it up. The skyline was hanging just off the ground and if we pulled in unison we could bounce the carriage and the cable sideways a little bit. Bob had to render the slack around the log as fast as he could and hold it there until the skyline finished swaying in the other direction. Then we pulled again.

I got behind Snow and started tugging. I couldn't see what was happening because I was stretched out nearly horizontal pulling on the choker with my back to them. "A little bit more," Bob grunted. When I heard the babbit slide into the bell I let up and turned around in time to see Snow jump on Bob's ass. He dry humped Bob a couple of times and yelled like a cowboy. Bob swung his arm back but Snow jumped back and laughed. Bob stood up and laughed too. "You're a logger now!" Snow said. As the words "What about me?" formed in my head they looked at me and sprang. Bob tackled me around the ankles and before I knew it he had me tied into a knot, butt up. "All right, some new fucking," Snow said as he slammed his hips onto my backside. It was definitely work place sexual harassment. He humped me a couple of times more before Bob let me up. "You're a logger now, too," Snow laughed. All three of us burst out laughing. We couldn't stop. Buffy stuck his head over the landing and yelled down to ask if we were all right. "THEY'RE LOGGERS NOW!" Snow's voice boomed up through the unit. Jed the Reb blew a long whistle from the yarder.

The rest of the day was fun. Except for pointing out what logs to choke Snow quit telling us what to do and we ran harder than ever. Slack off came a few minutes earlier than normal and when we jogged down the valley to the road, Snow stopped where I am standing now. Back then the stream bottom was surrounded by new clear cuts but a bend in the valley hid us from our landing and the road. Now, after 30 years of tree growth the spot is more secluded than ever. I was surprised to find a remnant of the trail, too, and I couldn't help follow it here for in many ways this is where the story I am telling was born. Had not what occurred here happened, Quiet Bob, Snow and myself may have gone our separate ways. We were right on Snow's heels and when he stopped he pulled out a big joint, lit it and handed it to Bob.

"I've never smoked wacky tobaccy," Bob said as he held the joint.

Snow finally exhaled. "That's what I figured. It's about time you found out why the man doesn't want you to."

"OK." He held the joint to his lips and sucked. As he passed it to me, he started coughing.

I took a hit and passed it to Snow, holding my breath. "That's good shit," I said when I let out a cloud of smoke. "It doesn't taste like Columbian."

Snow had taken another hit and passed it to Bob again. He let out his breath about the time Bob handed me the joint.

"It's not. It's sensimilla from northern California. Doesn't have any seeds. A friend of mine gave me a couple of big ounces for riding shotgun with him while he delivered a few pounds to Beverly Hills. Most of it's gone, but I have been saving the rest of it for a special occasion."

We passed the joint around. When it was almost a roach,

Bob let out with a big "Wow!" For the second time that day, our laughter echoed through the valley. When the roach was finally too small to pass, Snow swallowed it. We jogged the rest of the way to the road and got there as the crummy was pulling up. Everything was moving slow and I let myself drift with the high. I'd been smoking pot for years but can't say I was in love with it. I preferred booze and cocaine. Coke made me feel crazy. Pot was too mellow. But as I climbed into the back I realized I was part of this crew, part of the crummy, part of the yarder. I almost said, "Wow," too.

"I told you you'd enjoy getting stump broke," Buffy laughed as we sat down. "How'd it feel?"

I remember at the time it felt ridiculous. It's not like we were gay. Stump breaking was stupid. The pot on the other hand enhanced the feeling that I had just become a part of something bigger than myself.

"It's making me hungry," Bob replied to Buffy.

Even the loader operator and his assistant, Wing Tips, so named because he wore a pair of old dress shoes when not in his corks, thought that was funny but I doubt if they had a clue about the inside joke.

"Too bad it's Friday and the cookhouse is closed," someone said.

Months later, Quiet Bob told me that getting high for the first time after being stump broke was the most profound experience of his life. Up to then and for many years after, it was mine, too.

While walking from the yard to our bunkhouses, Snow told us that Jed had invited us down to his house in the village for a beer. After that if one of us wanted to drive to town he'd buy the first two rounds. We had to leave immediately though and couldn't take time to shower or change our clothes. We had to go in our rigging. That was fine with us.

Jed intercepted us in his yard. He said his wife was

45

mad at him and we couldn't come in but he had carried out four cold ones and after handing each of us one congratulated Bob and me for becoming loggers and making it on the crew. That left me speechless but Quiet Bob thanked him and said it was an honor to be working under his rigging. After a few more jokes while killing our beers, the three of us piled into my truck and I drove out of camp. Snow lit up another joint.

What a night. It was payday. Bob and I had small checks and cashed them at a bank. We weren't the only guys in work clothes. The Cub, the bar we went to, was full of loggers, sliver pickers from the mills, and Indians from the local reservations. Snow seemed to know everybody and everybody offered him drugs. By ten I was on my lips. It was the first of many such Friday and Saturday nights, about five years of them, spread out between Aberdeen, Olympia and Shelton.

We crashed at a house on Railroad Avenue where Snow's friend Pierre lived. Pierre was a French Canadian who worked at Grisdale once and now lived with a hippie gal named Kona. Bob slept on the couch and I slept on a big reel top table covered with carpet remnants. Snow was a regular there on the weekends and had a room upstairs. He didn't want to go to camp in the morning but Bob and I needed showers and clean clothes so we left. We stopped at a store and then headed for camp. He and I had gone in together on some good weed the night before so we had our own stash. For me, the pot took the edge off my hangover, but for Bob, every puff expanded his mind. We still had a few bucks in our pockets so after cleaning up and taking naps we headed back to town. We wound up in Bremerton that night at my friend Russ's place. The following spring I helped him get a job at Grisdale and he moved into Bunkhouse 11 with us.

The rig is only about a mile of easy walking from where the stream meets the road, so I don't have to hike up to the landing, thank god. If I had a joint, I would smoke it even though I haven't been high in several years. At least my beer is probably cold. There was still a lot of ice in the cooler this morning and I'm thirsty.

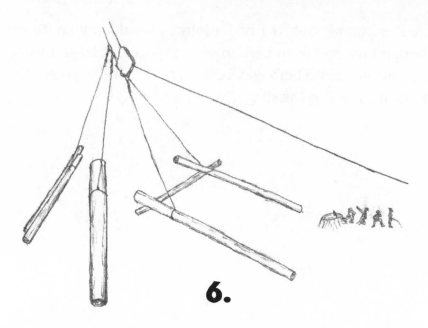

6.

Day 3, recorded while sitting on an old picnic table in a patch of sunlight at Wynoochee Falls.

After the walk yesterday, my body had trouble getting comfortable on the ground last night. I also had to pee more times than normal because of the five cans of beer I drank. I didn't fall sound asleep until it was almost dawn. When I opened my eyes, the sun was shining on the trees above me and the air was getting warm. I crawled out of the sleeping bag, stretched, boiled coffee and ate two bowls of grape nuts with raisins. While sitting on my cooler listening to the birds, I got the urge to drive to Wynoochee Falls for no other reason than to hear them.

I straightened up my gear and left it in camp this time. I drove slow along the lake with the window down. Nothing but war news was on the radio so I turned it off. Beyond the end of the lake, at the intersection with the road to the West Branch, I looked to the left and saw a truck parked near the bridge. I kept driving up the main stem, due north towards the boundary of the Olympic National Park. I was only going to the falls, I reminded myself.

The Forest Service has closed the campground. There is now a large wide spot along the road so I parked and killed the engine. Not a lot of water is flowing this time of year and the falls was barely a grumble. I sat in the rig a moment thinking about the good times we had up there. The one bad time was when Preacher and Acid brought a prostitute from town and set her up for business in a tent at this campground. A bunch of guys got VD.

I got out of the car and found the path down the hill alongside the dug up road. After just two steps a grey haired bear of a man bent over the handlebars of a mountain bike emerged from around a corner and almost ran me over. He was going slow though because he was headed uphill and I had time to hop to the side of the trail. He hardly looked at me and muttered, "Good Morning." That was when I recognized him. It was Big Dave, and he was the last person I wanted to run into.

Snow and he had set chokers together and were friends, but he had been a professional football player for a year or two before becoming a logger and I was probably jealous of that. What was he doing rubbing elbows with us losers? Of course, who was I to ask that question? But he carried himself like he knew he could beat any man up there and was pleased about it, plus we were competing with him and his crew and I had never been good at friendly competition.

Within three weeks, Snow, Quiet Bob and I were choking an average of 12 off highway logging truckloads a day. Big Dave and his chokermen on Slacker One was the only other rigging crew in camp who got as much but we were pulling away from them, too. After it became obvious that Snow wasn't going to run Quiet Bob and me down the road, Crank started sending other men into the brush with us. Some of them he wanted us to fire. A couple of guys quit when they

49

realized they were going to have to run all day. Those who could hang with us Crank put on crews that needed men. We never removed the fourth choker when we lost a man. Once we started, we flew four chokers whether someone was out there with us or not, and it was always full when it went up the hill.

That created problems. A union rule said that the company couldn't make a rigging crew use more chokers than there were men in the brush. That made sense but nobody was telling us to. It was our decision. Well, the truck drivers carried all the good and bad news of the day from the logging show to the transfer and from there to the other shows. The story spread that the three of us were trying to make every other crew look bad because we were using four chokers.

Crank knew he was in for a grievance but a controversy like this was entertainment for him. He never passed a chance to goad the less productive and more fatefully resigned members of the workforce he supervised. It took a couple of weeks for the issue to heat up but finally one day after work while us loggers were getting out of our crummies and heading home, the shop steward and another man went up to Snow and asked him why he was flying four chokers and whether or not he knew it was wrong. Snow just laughed and in his deep voice told them that if they thought it was unfair, they were welcome to come out with us and set it themselves. He'd love to have them.

"That's right, Snow, you tell'm," somebody from another crew yelled. The two men slinked away but that wasn't the end of it. Usually the union's business agent and company management took over at that point but thanks to me, it didn't get that far. The next day Bob and I were sitting in the cookhouse eating supper when Big Dave and two of his three chokermen came in late. Bob and I had taken showers before going over to the chow hall and Snow and most of the other men had already come and gone. Big Dave, Wayne and Frank were still sweaty and it was obvious they had put in some overtime. Dodge had kept their food warm. The three of them sat down on the other side of the table from Bob and me.

"How come you guys are late?" I asked, more to Wayne and Frank than to Big Dave. I had gotten to know them. They weren't bad guys. They worked hard on their crew just like Bob and I did on ours.

"We broke our skyline at two-thirty."

"That sucks." I replied as if I knew. We hadn't broken a cable on 7 since I had started logging. "How did you do that?"

"By trying to yard too big of a turn! How else do you part a skyline?" Big Dave jumped in. I should add here that later on Wayne told me Crank had just chewed Dave out for wooding down Slacker One. That machine would pull its guts out. Big Dave was already in a bad mood.

"Maybe you were flying too many chokers," I couldn't help from saying. Bob told me later that I did sound like a smart ass.

"Fuck you, Knucklehead," Big Dave shot back. Please note what he called me. "You think you're somebody special just because you're setting two chokers and making everyone else look bad. You couldn't pack shit on my crew!"

"Your shit's so thick that a man can't walk without stepping in it."

"You little twerp. I should take you outside and teach you a lesson."

That was my clue to back down, but no way could I do that.

"Okay. Let's go." I had to call his bluff, so I stood up.

Unfortunately, he stood up, too.

My instincts told me to spring over the table at him but Dodge intervened before I had a chance to. "Take it outside, gentlemen. There won't be any fighting in my cookhouse or

I'll see you both fired."

"Let's go," I said as I walked towards the door.

"Leave my food on the table, Bee. I'll be right back," I heard Dave say. Most of the men were laughing as I walked out and down the steps. I stepped off the boardwalk onto the lawn and turned around and watched Big Dave come out. He had been in his socks because a man couldn't wear cork boots in the cookhouse, and he stopped a moment on the porch to slip back into them.

"The trick is going to be to get in close where you can hit him but not let him grab hold of you," Bob said. He was standing next to me. A crowd had formed.

"This is going to hurt." I said to him.

"He probably won't kill you."

"Gee thanks."

Big Dave didn't take the time to lace his boots up all the way. He just wrapped the long leather threads around his ankles a couple of times and tied them into big bowknots. Thinking he was going to want to talk and dance around like Mohammed Ali, I launched into him the moment he stepped off the boardwalk onto the grass. That caught him by surprise. I managed to jab him in the face and when he raised his arms to protect himself, I hit him twice in the ribs, once on both sides. But that didn't move him. He had been hit a million times in the ribs and stomach by linemen a hundred pounds heavier than me. As he pushed me away, I got in one more lucky punch to one of his ears and I saw him wince as I caught myself from falling backwards.

Basically, by then, it was over for me. I danced in to try and jab him but his arms were a foot longer than mine, plus he had fast hands. I was able to block his first jab but his second one squared me on the side of the face below my left eye. I went in again and he landed two jabs to the face. That made me woozy, and when I tried to get inside his

52

reach a third time, my guard was down a little and he hit me on the jaw with a right. As I spun backwards onto my face, I saw stars. I don't remember hitting the ground. The next thing I knew I was lying on my arms and hands. My face was cocked sideways into the lawn. The cool grass was soothing on my injured cheek. On the other one I could feel the steel points of the nails on the bottom of one of Big Dave's boots. "I should give you a case of loggers' chicken pox," I heard him laugh. My mind was still detached from my body and it made no sense to me.

"Don't you dare," I heard Quiet Bob growl.

"What are you going to do about it?"

Dave's foot lifted as he stepped back and regained his balance. Bob ignored him and I felt myself being rolled over onto my back then lifted into a sitting position.

"You okay Ed?" my friend asked as he looked me in the eyes.

"Yeah, I'm okay," I replied. I could taste blood in my mouth and it was dripping out my nose.

"What bunkhouse do you live in?"

"Number 11, with you."

He stood me up and walked me over to the boardwalk, which was elevated a foot off the grass, and sat me down on the edge. Then he faced Big Dave. "It looks like I just did something about it."

"Maybe I should give you what I was going to give your bud."

"I'd ask you to go ahead and try but after we're done you might complain that you were already tired from fighting Ed. Maybe we should do it some other time when you're rested."

"Fuck you," he said and stepped towards Bob with his fists up. He jabbed at my friend as if he thought he was going to be able to do to Bob what he had done to me, but his arms were only six inches longer than Bob's and he only outweighed Bob by 25 pounds instead of 50. Bob crouched low with his forearms up in front of his face and bobbed and weaved towards his right like Smokin' Joe Frazier, deflecting most of the blows. A few got in but none of them hit him square. He threw a few punches back himself, and landed a couple too, but Big Dave kept his discipline and kept firing off left after left as he pressed towards Bob. Bob stepped into the barrage a couple of more times, threw some quick punches, and then retreated to his right. After they went around in a wide circle, Dave began spacing out his jabs while figuring out how to work them in through Bob's guard. As soon as he saw that happening, Bob stepped in with more force and delivered a low blow near Dave's groin. That had to be the most brilliant maneuver I have ever seen in a fight. He could have squared Dave in the gonads but he deliberately missed to the side. Dave went berserk. He started flailing towards Bob with big impressive roundhouses. Bob countered by stepping into Dave again, grabbing two fistfuls of Dave's hickory shirt, then turning his hip into the bigger man and throwing him over his back onto the ground. Some of the men watching cheered. Bob fell on Dave, twisted and rolled like a snake, and when they stopped moving, Bob was behind Dave, his legs were wrapped around Dave's, plus he had clamped his left arm under and around Dave's left arm so it was sticking uselessly into the air. His hands were also clasped together under Dave's chin and Dave was attempting to punch and reach backwards with his right arm but it was useless. My bunkmate had Big Dave in a death grip. The knuckles of Bob's left thumb were pressed against the big man's neck. Dave was looking up into the sky and everyone there could see the panic in his eyes as Bob squeezed. Let him loose, someone yelled, but nobody jumped down to help. A second or two later Dave's eyes started going blank. Just as his body went limp,

Bob let go and shoved Dave off. Dave took a big gulp of air then pushed himself to his hands and knees as he sucked in oxygen and coughed. Drool poured out of his mouth. It was a wonder he didn't choke but his head was hanging low to the ground like a dog's and he looked totally humbled. It was more than a defeat. Quiet Bob had handed him an identity crisis to deal with.

Bob and I didn't wait for Dave to get on his feet. We walked back to the bunkhouse and I lay down on my bed. The side of my face was throbbing. Bob told me he was going down to Jed's to get some ice. He came back a short time later with a bag of ice cubes and set it on my head.

"I wish I had a camera so I could take a picture of you right now," he said.

"Where did you learn to fight like that," I asked him.

"When I was a senior, I was the runner-up in the heavyweight division at the state wrestling tournament. I studied judo all the way through high school so I could be a better wrestler. I'm a black belt. The guy who beat me at state is going to the Olympics."

"That's the first time I have heard you brag," I said as he walked away. Several years later I saw more fighting like that in Brazil, but like they say, that's another story. In the short term at Grisdale, every once in a while I'd catch someone boasting how they had seen Quiet Bob take out Big Dave for beating the snot out of me. I usually kept my mouth shut. What could I say? Only 10 or 15 people had seen the fight but in a few weeks you would have thought everybody living and working in camp at the time had been there.

When I walked into the cookhouse the next morning, my face had ballooned out like a ruptured tire. I could barely see out of my right eye. My jaw was still in one piece but it was so sore I wasn't going to be able to chew any of Dodge's shoe leather for a week. While going through the chow line, the cook told Bob and me that Crank wanted to see us in the office at six-forty five sharp. I was convinced he was going to fire us, but Snow, who was already eating, told me that as long as we were there ready to work in the morning Crank would forgive us even if we killed everyone in Elma. "He'd make the cops come up to our show and arrest us as we were setting our last choker just to get every bit of sweat out of us he could." It's strange to think how prophetic those words were.

Big Dave had already been through the cookhouse and he was sitting in Crank's alcove office talking to the old man when we got there.

"Sit down, gentleman," the boss commanded as he nodded at the chairs his siderods and bull bucks usually sat in.

"I'm going to keep this short. I can't have my best men attempting to injure one another. So no more fighting after work, you got it?"

Yes sir, we agreed.

"And unfortunately there will be no more extra chokers on the butt rigging. I know that wasn't Big Dave's beef but the union pricks have already started whining to me about it and the little fight you boys had is going to give them ammunition to shoot at me. I've already talked to Ott about it. Enough said. One other thing, can you work today, Knucklehead? I think that's the biggest shiner I've ever seen. In fact I think I can see the imprint of Big Dave's fist tattooed on your cheek."

"Yeah, I can work, and I hope it's not tattooed." That broke the ice a little. Big Dave had a black eye too but it was nothing like mine, plus his ear had puffed up where I had cuffed him. But Crank didn't crack a joke about how easily Bob had incapacitated him. My feelings though were as expendable as ever. I could expect to be the brunt of his sadistic humor any time he saw me. Jed had called me Knucklehead for the first time a week earlier when I started ragging on Buffy for not filling the water bags, and thanks to a truck driver, Knucklehead had started following me like a lost dog. Now it was my name. Turneau told everyone that Crank gave it to me, which didn't make me happy. Jed even apologized to me for giving me the handle, but in reality, I liked it. My head did endure a lot of abuse, inside and out. I should be thankful that I can still remember who I am.

"Okay," Crank finished up. "I'm not going to do anything silly like make you guys shake hands. This isn't a Boy Scout camp. I don't care if you hate each other's guts. The harder you work to beat one another is fine with me so get out there and get some wood."

I've never been compelled to explore the concepts of fate and coincidence very deeply. What happens, happens. Sometimes it is amazing; sometimes it's a pile of shit, and that's about as religious as I get. Seeing Big Dave today though did make me wonder. We must have talked for an hour but didn't mention the fight until right before we went our separate ways. As we shook hands, he told me that the fight had been one of the best things that had ever happened to him and was a major turning point in his life. "Are you referring to the fight you had with me or the one with Quiet Bob?" I asked him. At long last we had something amusing to laugh about together.

(The sound of water falling over rocks.)

7.

Day 3.

I am back at camp now. The ice in my cooler has melted but the beer still tastes good. Plenty of daylight is left but clouds are blowing in from the ocean and the temperature has dropped. Rain is coming. If I had half a brain, I'd pack up and head for town. Instead, I built a fire and have a pile of wood, a blue tarp, and five more cans of warm beer. I should have invited Big Dave here for one after his ride.

My new friend's role in this story wasn't quite over. Grisdale had a sister camp called Govey, and a few weeks after the fight, the superintendent over there called Crank and asked if he had a good man at Grisdale who might want a hooktending job. Govey was a lot closer to Shelton and nobody lived there so it wasn't a real logging camp, but it actually had more yarders than Grisdale. Crank suggested Big Dave and my adversary left that night. The next morning, Hunt asked Bob if he wanted Dave's rigging slinging job on Slacker 1. Of course he did. I would have. After he walked over to Slacker 1's crummy, I got into our crew bus and slammed the door like a baby. Snow got in right behind me.

"That's fucked," he said. "I was hoping our crew would last the whole season. I was having fun kicking Dave's butt. And I liked all the sandwiches I bummed from Bob. But don't worry, Ed. I'm glad they left me you.

"Yeah," Buffy said as he climbed in behind our slinger. "He's saying he likes fucking you."

"That's right," Snow laughed. "I couldn't find the words to tell you so clearly. Thanks, Buffy."

"Fuck you guys." I looked away when I said that so it would be more difficult to see the slight smile on my face. Their jokes made me feel a little bit better but I was still pissed off.

Before we rolled out, Hunt took Buffy off the crummy. Buffy was a backup skidder operator and was needed somewhere. A few minutes later a guy named Elton got on the crummy. He was a career chokerman and was probably going to take Buffy's place. Then a college kid that Snow had stump broke a couple weeks earlier climbed in. As soon as we got to the landing, Ott jumped in the back.

"Ed, I want you to fill in on the landing for Buffy today. Elton hates to chase and Jed wants you up here with him today. I think it would be good for you, too. How about it?"

"I don't give a fuck what I do today."

"Good. Pay attention to Jed."

"And my sandwiches better not be squished when they come back at noon," Snow teased me. I screamed at Buffy any time the rigging banged up my lunch when it was shipped back at noon.

I hadn't missed a day in the brush in the two and a half months I had been there and didn't mind watching the rigging crew head into the hole without me. There wasn't much to unbelling chokers, and chasing that morning was easy. Ott didn't need any haywire in the tailend, so I didn't need to pull any sections off the haywire drum and make coils. That gave me plenty of time to stand there and pout. It also gave me the opportunity to watch how the rest of the show worked.

When the turns were coming in steady and there was a truck to load, the loader didn't stop twisting back and forth as Jersey Joe sorted through the new pile of logs on the landing and picked others out of the cold deck and set them on the truck. His machine sat on a turntable above tracks and it resembled a steam shovel only a huge set of grapples hung from cables at the end of the boom instead of a bucket. I could hardly believe how Joe could swing the loader and cast the grapples onto a log 30 or 40 feet away. I also appreciated how he tried to keep the landing cleaned off so I didn't have to scramble over logs to get to the ones I had to disconnect from the chokers. Normally he tried to set the ones with broken ends and limbs off to the side for Wingtips, but the second loader didn't hesitate to take his saw into the shoot and clean them up there while a turn was coming in. He seemed to have eyes in the back of his head and would step away right before Jed dumped the skyline. Of course Jed was watching him as well as Jersey Joe but it was still dangerous. I hated to think what could happen to him if one of the cables broke, but there were two chainsaws on the landing and in the afternoon I grabbed one of them and tried to help. Wingtips gave me my first lesson in operating a saw like a professional.

Jersey Joe didn't stop swinging logs unless there was some downtime or there weren't any trucks to load. I got a kick how the only time he became picky was when putting the peaker on top of the load. Sometimes he would try 2 or 3 different short fat butt cuts, turn them end to end and spin them around their centerline until he found one that fit and looked just right.

But like I think I said earlier, the yarder was the center

of attention and the man running it had the most important job on the landing if not the entire show. With wireworms zinging through the cables, the tower trying to shake loose from the guylines and the machine bucking like a beached whale, Jed looked as if he was having fun. He knew how to run the machine as close to the breaking point as possible. The bigger the turn the better. Like every other donkey puncher I knew, he enjoyed feeding as much diesel as he could into the turbocharged engine. When there was a break in the action during a road change, Jed slid the window of the cab open and invited me up onto the yarder, so I climbed the ladder and stood behind him while he waited for the next whistle.

"Are you still mad about Quiet Bob getting Big Dave's job?"

"Wouldn't you be?"

"Probably. For a little while at least, but you eventually need to stop letting it get you down."

"They fucked me! He almost went down the road the first day out. He's no better than I am."

"Hell, it's not going to be the first time in your life you get screwed over. I've been fucked lots of times. Besides, he's your friend."

"That makes it worse."

"Don't you think Crank asked Otto who he'd rather keep on the crew?"

"I bet he did. I bet they said let's fuck Knucklehead so he'll get mad and we can laugh at him."

"Then show the bastards you can handle it. Keep working your balls off like nothing is wrong. You are going to get your chance. You'll be a slinger, probably sooner than you think. You work harder than any man in camp. Crank knows that. Shit, I bet you'll be a hooktender someday."

"Right. You think so?"

"Sure do. You got hooktender written all over you. But

it's not easy and it's going to take a few years. And first you need to be a fucking slinger. I'm hoping that Crank doesn't take you off this crew before you pull rigging for me."

I was practically speechless. "What about Snow?"

"That crazy sonofabitch ain't called Snow for nothing. He can smell the white stuff coming in advance. In late November or December he'll disappear before it starts to fly. He'll go down to California and fuck his brains out and snort that other white stuff all winter. He won't show up again until sometime between March and May depending how broke he is."

"And Crank will hire him back?"

"Hell yes. In a heartbeat. Crank's not stupid. Snow is a good hand and he's good for the morale around here. When he takes off at the end of the season, that's when you'll get your chance. Make sure you know the whistles. I'll get Snow to let you pull rigging once in a while."

"I already know the whistles."

Before the end of the day he invited me down to his place that evening for a drink. "Bring your rigging pants with you, too. Maybe we can con Suzie Rae into patching them. Summer will soon be over and you won't need air conditioning down below to keep you cool."

I avoided Bob when I got into camp and walked down to Jed's. It was the middle of August and we sat in his backyard drinking bourbon and water until dark. Suzie Rae, his wife, hung out with us and drank a couple too as she sewed up the worst holes in my rigging. I was drunk when I got back to the bunkhouse. Quiet Bob was laying on top of his bunk reading *Sunset Magazine*. Yeah, *Sunset*. He had a subscription and liked to read about pots and pans, barbecuing, and kitchens. Every once in a while he'd tear out a recipe or a picture of a stove and stick it in a notebook. His dream was to build a house with a big kitchen. He looked up when I walked in.

"I'm sorry I acted like a baby," I told him. "You're my best friend. Congratulations for the promotion."

"Thanks," he said as he sat up and swung his feet to the floor. "I didn't realize you were upset. Where've you been?"

"Down at Jed's. He gave me a six-pack to share with you."

"Toss one over."

The abrupt stop in his fist caused the beer to foam when he popped the top. He had to guzzle half of it to keep from losing it on the floor.

"You think Snow wants one?"

"Probably. Let's go over and find out."

The remainder of that season played out like Jed said it would, except that Snow quit earlier than expected. He left on Halloween. The weather had been wet as hell but there was still a good month of work left before the snow would fly. He didn't say good-by to Quiet Bob or me. He got off the crummy in the evening, walked down to his bunkhouse, retrieved his sea bag which was already packed, and made it to the driveway out of camp in time to hop onto the Shelton bus. Bob and I talked about driving into town and having a beer with him but we figured if he had wanted to socialize he would have said something. "He'll be back in the spring," Jed told us the next morning in the yard. "And he'll have enough new stories to keep us entertained until the Fourth of July."

I started pulling rigging that day.

Jed covered up most of my mistakes and Ott showed a lot of patience. Crank didn't act very forgiving though. I was convinced he wanted an excuse to fire me and he never hesitated to let me know that he knew when I was fucking up. I got in trouble for leaving too many good logs in the brush then because I started sending too many culls to the landing. One week I broke three chokers and the blacksmith told me Crank told him not to give my crew and me any new ones for a while. Hell, Snow used to break chokers on purpose when they got too kinky or developed jaggers. Quiet Bob didn't have any trouble getting new chokers. It seemed like everyone enjoyed listening to me complain. I was a sideshow. I was entertainment. The chokermen that stuck with me did so because they liked to watch me get mad.

Most of them were scrawny local kids who liked to lie about the girls they had screwed, men they had beaten up, or jail time they had done for smarting off to cops. I didn't bust them if they did their jobs and only smirked as I ranted and raved. Only two of them spent entire seasons on my crew. Even my friend Russ didn't last long with me. In the middle of the summer of his first year, he got a job pulling rigging on Tower 5. Quiet Bob had a knack for training good chokermen. The harder he pushed them the more they liked it, and him. Men jumped at the chance to get on his rigging crew. I don't recall any man asking to work with me but eventually the mechanics of the job became second nature, and Jed and I got to where we knew what each other was thinking before I blew a whistle.

I need to take a break.

Jed was in his early thirties when he came to camp and began logging. That was old for a chokerman but Sprint told us Jed kicked butt, earned lots of respect, and became a rigging slinger. A year later he busted his leg. After he healed, Crank put him on the landing chasing. Not long after that he started running yarder. By then his wife had caught up to him and she and Jed got a house in the village. What do you mean by "caught up with you?" I asked him.

"I was in some trouble back home and had to leave in a hurry."

"What did you do?"

"I don't like to talk about it. I didn't hurt anybody though. It had something to do with selling stolen cars but all that stuff is behind me. I'll always appreciate Crank for giving me a fresh start. Don't say anything about what I just told you, okay?"

There was no more discussion about his past or Suzie Rae. However, Snow told me that Jed told him that he had left his first wife for Suzie back in the small town in North Carolina where he got in trouble. It was no secret that Jed was a Tar Heel. Nobody knew where Suzie was from though. She didn't talk southern and Bob said he heard Jed refer to her as a carpetbagger. So that was about all we knew, which was about as much as we knew about anyone up there, and a lot more than what people knew about me.

People could build their own identities at camp and leave it behind as soon as they moved on. Everybody at Grisdale thought Suzie Rae was a saint for putting up with Jed's drinking and an angel for the support she gave her neighbors. They could rely on her for a ride to town or picking up things when she went in alone. When kids started sleeping over at Suzie's and Jed's, everyone knew their parents were about to break up. She also volunteered at the one room grade school, one of the last in the state.

At a meeting, the young couple that taught there told the community how the children would benefit from having a television in the room. That got a few laughs because the big antenna on top of an old fir tree only allowed us to watch two of the three national networks broadcasting out of Seattle. The teachers explained how a "dish" could be put up on top of Weatherwax and the TV signals brought down to camp via a cable. The school could then subscribe to a service that would provide educational programs. The equipment would cost about $15,000, which was more than most loggers made in a year back then. Everyone thought that was too much money but when the teachers told them that all the houses could patch into the new system too and for a monthly fee have reception as good as anyone in town, the idea suddenly became popular, and Suzie Rae volunteered to lead a fundraising campaign.

The people in the village knocked themselves out at first but when it became clear that the bake sales, raffles and car washes weren't going to be enough, Suzie began soliciting funds directly. Everybody said that Jed had the best looking wife in camp but whenever I saw her she stayed in the background. A lot of men wished they had wives like that, too. However, when she started raising funds, a new Suzie emerged. She was hard to say no to. Skoot, who was still new to camp, swore that when she confronted him outside the cookhouse one evening, he towered up (got an erection) even though while she was speaking, he was thinking how she looked like one of his eight year old daughter's friends. He said he couldn't recall one word she told him yet he pulled out his wallet and handed her a 50. By talking face to face with every wage earner in camp, including all us deadbeats in the bunkhouses and the drones riding the buses to and from town everyday, she raised half of what was needed. That primed the pump. Her next move was to put together a list of the businesses the company bought supplies from and to start going to town herself every day.

Jed told me that made him nervous. Do you think she's fooling around, I asked? Could be something like that, he answered. He didn't sound like a man who was concerned that his wife was screwing other men. Or was he just acting cool? When she traveled to Seattle and spent two nights there, Jed turned into a nervous wreck. She came back and said she had talked to the "cable company," a new term back then. She claimed they agreed to install the dish, cable and other electronic components for almost half the price of what they quoted the school teachers. On top of that she had also talked to the Department of Education in Olympia and they offered the school district a grant for $2,000.

Two days later Suzie disappeared. Jed drove up to the office in the morning and talked to Crank in private. We knew something was up because they didn't come out until after 7 am. All the other crew buses left and we sat in the crummy staring down at the office. When they finally did appear, they jumped into Crank's pick up and drove out the other side of camp towards town. Hunt came over and told Ott that he was going to have to run yarder that day. Hunt also told us that Jed suspected Suzie had taken the money she raised.

We heard later, from Jed no less, that when they got to the bank they found $7,000 in the account, which was about the amount of money the people of Grisdale had raised collectively. The account records indicated that Suzie had come in the day before and withdrew $56,000. Originally, just Crank's name was on the bank account and Suzie had only been able to deposit the donations. The previous week though, Crank had been gullible enough to put her name on the account, too. After going to the bank, they went to the company's office in Shelton and then to the sheriff's office. To top it off, she had also withdrawn $30,000 that she and Jed had saved to buy a piece of property and build a house with, but the sheriff told him that was community property and a civil matter.

Jed was still spitting nails when he wandered drunk into our bunkhouse that evening and told us the story. "She's a smooth bitch," he said over and over again. "A real smooth bitch. I should have known she couldn't change." He wouldn't answer the questions we asked and as his anger subsided, he fell into despair and then cried himself to sleep on the spare bunk.

Grisdale ran on gossip. Everybody knew or thought they knew one another's dirty laundry, especially down in the village. The main theory was that Jed masterminded the scam and was staying put until winter shutdown when he was going to disappear quietly and join Suzie. He wished that were true. "I still love her, but I'll never see her again. She's too smart for that, and heartless."

There were plenty of theories. The one I liked was that Crank had been working with her. One logger's wife claimed she had seen Crank and Suzie kissing in the parking lot at Taylors, a restaurant south of Shelton. That got a laugh but then two FBI agents drove to Grisdale and arrested Jed. Their investigation had uncovered details of his past, too. Both had been wanted in North Carolina for an auto theft scam nine years earlier. Because Suzie hadn't joined Jed until he had been at Grisdale for a few years, her rap sheet was fresher and more extensive than his. The statute of limitations had also expired and the government would have had a hard time prosecuting him for his crimes. When he returned, he said he had told the FBI everything he knew about Suzie but that most of what he knew about her were lies. "They'll never find her and if they do the money will already be gone." I remember hearing him say that a dozen times. He was crushed and sympathy quickly replaced the entertainment value of the rumors.

Before Suzie left, his pattern was to drink most heavily during the winter when camp was down, then sober up in the spring. As the days got longer and warmer, he'd start drinking beer at night and by the Fourth he'd be back on the hard stuff. He knew his limit though and never came to work drunk or so hung-over he couldn't drive the crummy and stay awake in the yarder. Several lives, mine included, were in his hands and he took that responsibility seriously. His greatest fear was that he would kill somebody in the rigging.

I never worried about it until after Suzie split. A couple of mornings he came to work so screwed up that Ott sent him home. Then Crank had a talk with him, which seemed to help. Being a single guy all of a sudden, he had to vacate his house in the village, so he moved into a bunkhouse inhabited longer than anyone could remember by a tough old faller and a changing cast of middle age, long term employees. Like Skoot said, camp was a halfway house for men running or recuperating from women. Although none of them were teetotalers, Jed found some restraint there. I still had reason to be nervous though while setting a turn and blowing for him to go ahead easy on the mainline. I tried to blow in the whistles a little slower than normal to make sure he heard them clearly. Having been in sync with him for so long, I was afraid he and I would lose the ability to anticipate what the other was going to do. I don't know. Maybe it was me who had lost a sliver of faith in him, but I had the feeling he no longer had confidence in himself, which was understandable.

Things came to head during a cold wet August day on The Burn. In 1974, lightning started a fire in steep rocky ground on the east side of Lake Wynoochee. The wind carried sparks across the lake and started a bigger blaze in similar ground on the west side. It was a hot fire and killed all the timber it got into. The word was that since the trees were dead, logging them was a salvage operation and the Forest Service was giving the timber to the company for free. Whatever, they should have paid us twice the wages to cut and yard it since the terrain was so gnarly. The side of the ridge it burnt was a series of cliffs. The ravines in between and the bowls below the cliffs had been full of Doug fir old growth with bark thick enough to protect the beautiful wood inside. There was no way the yarders could pick the big logs high enough to clear the top of the rock faces and when the turns hit them and were dragged over the rims they knocked loose boulders the size of Volkswagens. Not only did we have to run for our lives at least once a day, all the underbrush and duff had been seared away and scrambling over the hard broken ground chewed the nails and leather off the bottom of our boots. The company logged four shows on The Burn and I pulled rigging on three of them. Quiet Bob only had to log one.

Anyway, while finishing up the last show on The Burn, we accidentally flopped the carriage around the skyline and burned a bad spot into our mainline. Luckily it was near the end of the cable so all we had to do to fix it was cut off 30 feet of line and splice a new eye. That was easy. I always enjoyed splicing. From unshackling the mainline to shackling it back to the carriage, a good crew could do the job in 45 minutes on a bad day.

Since we were on the Burn, nobody cared about production. Plus, it was a cold wet summer day. The wind was howling as if it was November or March, so spending one less hour in the brush was fine with us. We would have stretched the task to two hours if we could. Jed was the only man on the crew who seemed annoyed by the down time. He was fidgety as hell as he watched us splice and in today's terms I could tell he was jonesing for a drink. He was happy as hell to see us head over the landing when we were done.

The skyline was still slacked all the way to the valley bottom. For the first hundred yards below the landing, the big cable sat a few feet off the ground allowing us to hold onto it as we ran down the hill. In fact we had been doing that for the past couple of weeks because the steep slope above the first cliff was so clean from dragging logs across it for two months. When we got to the top of the rock, we would veer off to a narrow shoot that descended to the pockets of felled timber below. That morning though when we were halfway to where we turned to the side, Jed started winding the cable in. That was totally against the rules. When men were in the brush, the yarder engineer couldn't move a cable without being told to by a whistle or hand signal.

We automatically let go of the cable and started running to the side. I also sent in one whistle to stop him from cabling up any more but the whistle didn't blow. He hadn't turned them on that morning and I hadn't tested them before heading down the hill. It wasn't particularly dangerous yet. We had plenty of time to get to the side and let Jed figure it out. I was pissed off though so I turned to scream "Turn on the whistles you drunken bastard," knowing he wouldn't be able to hear me, but thank God I did because I saw a short broken log skipping over the stumps like a torpedo aimed straight at my head. I had just enough time to relax my legs and fall backwards. The log passed so close I could feel the displaced air brush my face. Had it hit me my skull and its contents would have been spread over the hillside like a smashed pumpkin.

When he saw the skyline kick the log off the edge of the landing, Jed tried to blow a long string of short blasts as a warning. That's when he discovered the whistles were turned off. He quit going ahead on the skyline and shut down the machine. Buffy looked over the landing. I had sprung back to my feet and was already headed up the slope. With the machines off, the guys up there could hear me coming. Jed had gotten out of the yarder and was standing on the ground when I got to the top. Seeing him ready to get his head chopped off brought me to my senses. I think I would have been doing him a favor if I had gone over and clobbered him but instead I took my whistle off, threw it onto the ground, picked it up, put it back on, then headed back down the hill. That must have been a comical sight but I didn't hear anybody laugh.

Even though I shared some of the blame, this incident

had more of an effect on him than it did me. He decreased his alcohol consumption to a safe level after that and ran yarder like his old self. However, a short time later he put in for a job on the falling crew. Crank gave it to him under two conditions: one, that he teach Buffy how to run yarder, and two, that he go to rehab and dry out. He gladly did both. Breaking in Buffy took longer than his trip to Happy Valley.

Jed came back looking good. He loved working in the brush again. Packing a chainsaw put ten pounds of muscle on him the first month. That winter he didn't drink a drop of booze. He moved out of the bunkhouses into a trailer on Lake Nahwatzel and found a girlfriend. Things were going right for him, he said, for the first time in a long while. But you could see the black cloud following him. That next summer a widow maker hit him in the head while he was falling a tree and he died in a stretcher on an old landing waiting for a helicopter to carry him to the hospital. The news of death blows through the woods like a cold wind. It is passed from logger to logger quietly with sadness and the tone of finality. I was stunned. Did my father have friends who felt as bad when he died, I wondered?

We shut down Tower 7 and drove to camp. The ambulance was still parked outside the office so we joined the crowd of men that had gathered around it. Jed was strapped to the gurney in back in a body bag under a blanket. I swear I could feel his presence hovering there with us. Finally, Turneau came out of the office and along with Boris, the shop foreman, climbed into the meat wagon and carried our friend away. There was nothing left to do but go down to the bunkhouse, get drunk and tell stories about him.

His people came out from North Carolina to take him home. We had a service for him before they left. How Suzie Rae heard about it was anybody's guess. She sent a bouquet of flowers that dwarfed all the others in the little church. I didn't know whether to be happy or angry about that but thinking she might be crying gave me some satisfaction. The Lord knows he loved her until the day he died.

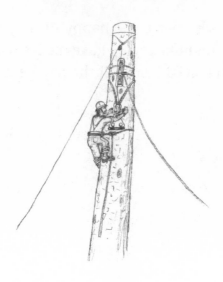

8.

Day 3, in camp, late, before midnight.

One thing I have learned coming up here is that growing old would be even less appealing if I had to sleep on the ground and climb to my feet and stand in the rain to relieve myself a couple of times every night. It's not coming down hard yet, but it is dripping off the trees I am under and to top it off my shoulder has started hurting. It usually does when the weather turns bad. I've been laying here for an hour with my eyes closed massaging myself trying to drift off. What's really fucked is that my Ibuprofen is in the truck and I have to walk out and get it.

I just took three tablets and am back in my sleeping bag. It will take them a while to kick in. The pain makes me think about getting busted-up, which makes me think about going to Mexico with Bob and Snow, which then makes me think about meeting Ruby.

That was in the spring of 1979. My '56 Chevy pickup was stolen outside of Cabo and when I got back to Seattle, I had to buy a new truck, a Silverado 4x4. As I drove it to Grisdale

I thought about how I finally needed to resolve my questions about my father's death. However, as before, those thoughts quickly disappeared when I got to camp, this time when I walked into the office and saw Ruby. She was sitting at the desk behind the counter. Her blouse I swear was unbuttoned down to her navel and it was obvious that she had the nicest breasts I could imagine.

"Can I help you?" She looked up and asked.

I tried not to dwell on her dark hair, high cheekbones and Native American perhaps Latina brown eyes.

"Is Turneau around? The doctor just released me to come back to work, and I want to get the paperwork over with."

"I can probably help you with that. What's your name?"

She stood up. The curves of her body looked like ski tracks in fresh powder snow. She had on a short skirt and dark stockings. Without seeing her from the rear I could tell she had a nice one. Her dark hair bounced slowly about her shoulders like slinkies. However, the smile on her lips and the glow in her eyes are what lit me up the most.

"Ed Knockle."

"You're Ed the Head?" she almost squealed. "I've heard so much about you. I see why they call you Knucklehead." She said that as if my nickname was a title of honor. "Can I touch it?"

"You can rub it if you want to," I said as I leaned over the counter.

"That feels nice," she said, as she traced her fingers along the faded scars.

"No shit," I said and we both laughed.

Turneau then walked into the room. Luckily I had stood back up. Ruby had uncanny timing.

"Well Mr. Knucklehead," he greeted me. "Where's The Cowboy?"

"He's in California."

"I guess Sprint wins that bet. A few weeks ago we were speculating when you two would return. Sprint said he didn't think you would show up together and that you'd get here first. He even predicts that Snow will drag his behind back in here. I hope so. It's more fun when he's around."

Snow hadn't worked at Grisdale in a couple of years. He quit after refusing to take a hooktending job Crank offered him in front of everyone one morning. Everybody would have fought to work on his crew, but he wanted no part of being a boss and when Crank got frustrated and insinuated there was something wrong with his character, Snow got pissed and told him he didn't need that kind of bullshit, then walked off. He went up to Forks, then Alaska, the motherland of logging tramps. Nobody heard from him again except for Quiet Bob because both of them liked to write letters. I knew Turneau would love more information about my friends so I didn't give him any.

"I see you already met Ms. Faulk. She's our new secretary. I'm sure glad the company hired somebody to help me. I've been swamped with work ever since Gladys retired. Headquarters has given us a big quota this year."

I ignored my urge to say something cynical. "Do I have to sign any papers to go back to work?"

"No, but you need a release from a doctor. Officially you are still injured."

I unfolded the note from my doctor and laid it on the counter. "It says I'm released to full duty."

Turneau picked it up and read closely. He had a skill for finding mistakes he could wave in our faces then fix. "You're right," he said as he nodded his head. "Wait here and I'll radio Crank to find out if he wants you to show up tomorrow morning. We haven't called all the crews back yet."

"I hear your shoulder was smashed really bad," Ruby

76

said as soon as Turneau left the room. "How is it now? Does it still hurt?" Her expression had changed to one of concern.

"It hurts a little but I'm back to full strength. I still don't have my entire range of motion though."

"Maybe I can help with that. I've studied therapeutic massage. Will you let me work on you? I need the practice."

"Maybe," I mumbled.

Turneau walked back in, laughing. "His exact words were, 'Hell yes! I have five yarders going and only two slingers at the moment who know that a bonus is extra logs instead of extra pay.'"

"I'm serious," Ruby told me.

I was smiling when I walked out. I drove my truck back around to the parking sheds and carried my laundry basket to the bunkhouse unable to believe they had hired a woman as hot as her to work in a camp full of horny loggers. Perhaps it was a scheme to harass us. At least my bunk was vacant. So was Bob's. Russ's rigging was in his corner. He had been dating a 35-year-old accountant when we left and didn't want to go to Mexico with us. He and the crews would be getting back in an hour. I lay down on my bunk and closed my eyes. The old bed felt good. A little while later I awoke listening to men stomping down the boardwalk and talking. Some I recognized and some I didn't. It was a new season.

The rain is falling hard now and the wind is blowing. Each blast shakes a heavy sheet of water off the trees onto my camp. One hit me a few moments ago when I got up to pee. Luckily I had folded the tarp back over my bag and getting doused once wasn't so bad. It actually felt good to be standing in the damp, stirred up air. As I shook the dew off, I looked into the black night for ghosts half expecting to see one. I threw most of the wood on the fire and crawled back into the bag. The pain in my shoulder has receded to a dull ache.

It was good to see Russ. He had played in the secondary with me on the football team at Olympic and we knew each other well. I went to the cookhouse with him for supper. Everyone wanted to hear about Mexico, so I told them Snow had met a beautiful woman and decided to go further south with her. The last time we saw him was at the ferry from La Paz to Mazatlán. Bob and I stayed on Baja and went deep sea fishing as planned. We caught lots of Dorado and tuna and Bob hooked and landed a Striped Marlin. I pulled the photo out of my wallet of the two of us standing next to the dead fish hanging upside down on shore. Skoot wanted to know if we fucked any women and I lied about that, too. He was disappointed I didn't have any pictures of them.

"So where's Bobs?" he asked.

"Still in California." I explained how my truck was stolen and how we then flew up to Los Angeles with the last of our money and dropped in on my cousin Robert. Robert worked in Hollywood and at the time was an assistant art director on a football movie called "Grid Iron Crucible." He actually got us jobs in it too, Quiet Bob as slightly more than an extra on the football field playing a linebacker and me, because of my bum shoulder, doing grunt work behind the scenes. Bob was still down there filming but I got bored and quit and came back alone. There was more to the story, like how I flew to my mom's place in Puerto Vallarta and did push-ups and pull-ups every day for two weeks to get my shoulder back in shape, and how Robert was gay and had a crush on Bob, but they didn't need to know those things.

The next morning I went to the office and told Crank that I wanted a promotion. I figured I was due. Every once in a while, if Tower 7 wasn't on a tough show, he'd give me a temporary assignment on a crew that needed a slinger as dumb as me. Jed said it was a sign of respect but it felt like punishment. I had done his dirty work for four years.

Now I wanted to work in the tailend. I wanted to become a hooktender.

"You want to do what?" he laughed. "Look, Knucklehead, I can't put you in the tailend. I need men in the rigging who know what they are doing. I'm trying to get this place fired up for the year. We have a large quota this go around."

I didn't say anything.

"Okay. Here's the deal. Keep this under your hat, okay?" He leaned forward on his desk and talked a little quieter although everyone in the office must have known what was going on. "Tomorrow I am shaking things up. I've got a new hooktender coming in and I'm giving him Tower 7."

"What's Ott going to do?"

"My brother is happy. We gave him the bid on the falling crew he wanted. There's more though. The new hooker is bringing a yarder engineer and a slinger with him, too, along with a couple of other men."

I didn't ask where Buffy was landing. We were all Crank's pawns.

"Who is this new hooker? He must be something special."

"Oh he is," Crank smiled. "It's Spike Larue. He is the best damn hooktender we have ever had up here."

I'd heard stories about him, none of them good. Everyone said he was a prick. When I came to camp, he was in prison for robbing a bank. Apparently, he was out now.

"I still want to work in the tailend."

"I'll keep it in mind. When things are running smooth, maybe we'll need a second rigger somewhere and if I can I'll put you there."

Nearly every man in camp claimed that Crank had double-crossed him at some point and I knew his half-baked promise was the best I was going to get.

"Where do you want me today?"

79

"On 7. The slinger quit yesterday when I told him I was giving his job to Spike's man. He wasn't worth a shit anyway."

"Great. Buffy gets another chance to kill me."

"This will give you two a chance to patch things up."

I walked out of the office and up to the yard.

To be fair to Buffy, he wasn't that bad of a yarder engineer. And he and I had already patched things up. He had blamed himself for my accident but it was just as much my fault as it was his. The morning it happened I had given him shit for being too easy on the rigging. On the very first turn, I choked a pecker pole sticking out of a pile of brush that turned out to be a long stick, meaning the faller had forgotten or been unable to buck it into logs. Buffy punched it hard. Before I could stop the rigging, the log nosed into a stump, swung around like a bat and whacked me in the shoulder. Turneau finally got to drive me to town in the ambulance.

Spike and his gang came in about 10 pm and clomped down the boardwalk like they were drunk.

"This place hasn't changed in seven years." That had to be Larue. "Don't make any noise. It looks like all the boys are in bed and if you wake them up they might come out and pound us." His buddies laughed. They stumbled past my hootch down to the other end of the bunkhouses. I could hear them for an hour or so opening and slamming doors, walking back and forth to the latrine and parking lot. One of them started hollering and Larue barked at him to shut up. "Go to bed. Tomorrow you need to show the boss you can work. He'll fire your ass if you can't. Hell, I'll run you down the road if you embarrass me. You perverts are going to need all the juice you can muster." Things quieted down after that.

In the morning at the cookhouse, I was disappointed to see that physically he wasn't impressive. Those were the worse kind of bullies. The way he talked through clenched

80

teeth made him sound bigger than he was.

Crank put me on Tower 2. That was okay. Skoot was the yarder engineer and he was as good as Jed had been. He drank as much as Jed, too.

That evening, Larue and his crew were already in the cookhouse when I got there. They looked tired and ragged and weren't talking much. Apparently, over in Morton they had been working on smaller hi-lead shows. Larue had spent most of the day "teaching" them how to shotgun and he was still giving them lectures. Then Ruby walked in.

"There you are," Larue switched subjects. "Come sit with me when you get your food. I ain't ever eaten in here with a pretty woman."

She didn't hesitate. "No thank you, Spike," she said sweetly and smiled at him. "Most nights I sit with Ed and his friends and I think I'd miss their company."

That was news to me, especially since I had only been there a day.

"We don't bite," he said.

"I'm not sure Ed and his friends can say that," she replied real quick, causing us all to laugh.

"Well, if that's what it takes . . ." but nobody was listening to him anymore. We were watching Ruby and waiting to see if she was actually going to sit with us, which she did, next to me.

"How are you doing, Ed," she asked. "How's your shoulder?"

"Fine," I said.

She made as much conversation as she could but for the most part it made everyone nervous and Russ, Skoot, FDR, Junior, and whoever else was there got up one by one and left.

"Please stay with me until they're gone," she whispered.

I nodded my head. "Thanks," she said, when Spike and his crew finally left.

"You're welcome." I stood up to leave.

"I meant it about massaging your shoulder."

"I haven't forgotten the offer."

"I won't let you."

"Good, keep reminding me."

The next morning, Larue came up to me while I was making sandwiches.

"You and Ruby pretty tight?" He didn't bother with introductions.

"Not really."

"So you're not getting a piece of that pussy of hers?"

"No."

"Then you won't mind me making a play for it myself I take it."

"Go for it if you think you have a chance."

"Ain't nobody up here fucking her?"

"Not that I know of."

"She sure has some knockers on her."

"Yeah, I wouldn't mind rubbing my face in them." I regretted saying that. I wanted to tell Larue that he didn't have a chance, that she wasn't there for him, me, or anyone else in camp at that moment. I knew who she was waiting for even though she didn't know it herself. I was waiting for him, too. I wanted to see the look on Larue's face the first time he saw Ruby look at Quiet Bob.

The next day, Larue came up to me again.

"Crank told me you're the best rigging slinger in camp."

"That's news to me."

"He said that he'd transfer you to my crew if you wanted."

"He's never given me any options like that before. What's wrong with that guy you brought?"

"He's a hi-lead man. It's going to take him a while to get the hang of shotgunning and I'm guessing that he won't

82

be worth a shit when we begin to slackline. I want the best rigging crew I can get."

"Thanks for the offer but I like where I'm at."

"You like working for Mel?" Mel was my hooker.

"Yeah. Mel and I get along. And the engineer and I are friends."

"Sounds like a happy crew. I'd hate to break it up. You fucked Ruby since I last talked to you?"

"Yeah, right, I wish."

"You better hurry. She'll be useless when I get done with her," he laughed.

"In your dreams," I replied, looking at him in the eyes. "And I bet they are wet ones." I hadn't felt like fighting at the drop of a hat in a long time.

He pretended to wince and look hurt. Then he chuckled and walked off towards the office. He never asked me to work on his crew again.

However, his interest in my relation to Ruby did water a seed. Not long after that, probably that very night after turning the lights out, the idea arose that maybe I did have a chance with her, and if so, I better take it before Quiet Bob came back to camp. I knew I'd be an idiot if I didn't let her give me a massage.

A few days later she walked into the cookhouse looking depressed. She sat close by and after the other men left I told her my shoulder hurt and was willing to let her work on it. That made her smile. She told me to take a shower and come to the office at eight o'clock. That was kind of strange. I was expecting to be invited to her bunkhouse.

What if somebody walked in while we were balling, I wondered? A man could dream. When I walked up there, I saw that the shades on the office windows were drawn and anybody strolling by wouldn't be able to see in. Some guys were standing down near the latrine talking, so I circled around until they disappeared then darted onto the office porch and tried the door. It was unlocked and she was sitting at her desk going through timesheets.

"Where do you want to do this," I asked immediately.

"Right here on the counter," she smiled, her eyes twinkling.

"Really?"

"Yes. It's perfect. Here, you can put your head on this pillow. I've been sitting on it all day, but don't worry, I put some perfume on it."

"So your butt doesn't actually smell this good," I asked on impulse.

She laughed hard. "I wish," she said and walked over to the door to lock it.

"Hop up there," she told me. "Take your shirt off . . . Lay back."

She poured massage oil on her hands and rubbed them together.

"Do you have training in this?" I asked.

"I do. I took a class in massage therapy so I could massage my husband when he came home from work."

The rumor was that the guy worked in the oil fields and was currently on a job someplace in the Middle East. According to her, she was in the process of divorcing him.

"I'm going to start on your head," she said before laying her hands on me. "Now close your eyes and relax."

I shut up and let her get started. Nobody had ever rubbed my head like that. I think it was the first time I actually appreciated having no hair. She massaged my eyes, nose and ears. Then she hit the muscles in my jaw. By the time she got to my neck my whole skull felt detached. I barely noticed when she moved down to my chest. Thank God I had my jeans on. She massaged my good shoulder then walked around to the other side and started on my bad one. Her touch was light at first but then got heavier and more focused.

"I can feel the scar tissue in there. Does it hurt?"

"A little but it feels good, too."

"Do you mind if I apply more pressure?"

"Go for it."

As well as breaking a few bones, the log had ripped ligaments between my muscles and arm. Ruby put her forearm right over the most sensitive area and leaned down hard as she circled her elbow over my soft tissue. The pain traveled all the way down to my ass but I almost moaned with pleasure. She followed the scar down my bicep. Her hair had fallen onto the skin of my wound, too, and was brushing it softly. I could feel the breath from her nostrils. I could smell her and opened my eyes. The look in hers was intense. I never could have admitted it at the time but I was totally awed by the depth of caring they revealed. She smiled and I closed my eyes again. That made it easier not to think about kissing her.

A few moments later she had me turn over and began working on the other side. By then I was completely into it. Was I the luckiest guy in camp or what? She found a kink in the small of my back and her fingers slipped under my belt towards my crack as she worked on it. That sent a charge straight through my pelvis. As she worked back up my spine towards the shoulder where she would perform the grand finale I opened my eyes slightly. It took a moment or two to realize what I was looking at.

File cabinets. Big deal. They were kind of blurry. Then my eyes focused on a label. "Lost Time Injuries, 1965-69." My eyes followed the drawers down one file cabinet and up the next. The top two drawers were labeled differently. I didn't have to squint to read the label on the second one down, "Fatalities, 1960-." The one above it, the top drawer said, "Fatalities, 1946-59." The answers to most of the questions I came to Grisdale with were a few feet away from me squeezed between the covers of a manila file with my father's name on the tab.

"What happened?" Ruby asked. "Did I hurt you?"

"No. I have to go to the bathroom."

"That happens. Massages loosen things up. Do you want me to stop so you can relieve yourself?" She could be such a lady.

"No, keep going."

"I'll hurry. I should have started on your back first."

When she was finished, I sat up and put my shirt on. "That was great. It feels a lot better," I told her as I swung my arm and shoulder around slowly. "You could make a fortune up here."

"Please don't tell anyone. I'm only going to do this for you. Let's keep it a secret, okay?"

"Don't worry. My lips are sealed."

"Does it really feel better?"

"Yes, it does. You have magic fingers."

"That's so sweet of you to say. Thank you."

I could use one of her massages now. The rain has almost snuffed out my fire. It's pitch black out. I'm going to pull the tarp over my head and try to sleep.

9.

Day 4, starting in camp.

It's getting light. I didn't sleep much. Every time I drifted off a rain shower woke me up. I stayed fairly warm and dry under my tarp but the view of my soaked camp from here is depressing. No way am I going to try and build a fire.

I'm in the Yukon now. All my gear is piled in back. I'm wet and dirty and tired of eating hot dogs and peanut butter sandwiches. I need to check into a motel and clean up. Tomorrow I go to the sheriff's office and late the next night I head back to South America. I don't know if I am going to have time to finish the story. (There is a long pause. You can hear the engine running, the fan, a DJ mumbling on the radio.) Warm air is finally blowing from the heater and drying the fog off the windshield. I'm heading to Shelton for breakfast.

Now it's late afternoon. I am clean and have taken a nap. On the way to town I stopped at the Matlock Store for coffee. That was the closest place to camp where we could buy beer, tobacco and gas. The old store was closed but still standing and a new one stood behind it. A couple of old men

I didn't recognize sitting at a table watched me like a couple of wary crows as I filled a Styrofoam cup with coffee and paid the new proprietor. Shelton used to be a two-beer drive from Matlock. Twenty-five years ago this road was buried in second growth trees too but they're gone now and I had to look at the bleak grey sky the whole way in. Along the way the Lake Nahwatzel Resort looked shut down, and in Shelton, driving down Railroad Avenue, I saw that Pierre and Kona's hippie house had been demolished. The lot was vacant. The Pine Tree was still in business though. It was right outside the gate to the mill, and the dark bar in back had been our first stop after the bank on Fridays. I just went into the restaurant for breakfast. Nobody that I knew came in which made me feel lonely, so I left and got on the freeway to Olympia. I was thinking about driving all the way to Seattle to catch one of the last Mariner baseball games of the season and staying at my mom's, who was in Hawaii. She had sold the casa in Vallarta and bought a place on Maui, but south of Shelton I saw the new casino at the Kamilche Cutoff. The hotel was nice looking and had to be the tallest building in the county. I turned around at the next exit and here I am.

That was several hours ago and I'm at a table in one of the casino bars. I put the earphones on that came with the recorder and am pretending to be having a phone conversation.

The place is crowded even though it's a weeknight. Football and baseball games are playing on big screens. Advertisements for cage fights and concerts by aging pop stars are flashing on others. Everyone is smoking, too. I guess the Indians don't have to follow the state's anti-smoking laws so their gambling enterprises give nicotine addicts a place where they feel loved. The smoke-free craze hasn't hit South America yet so I'm still used to it. The background music is about to drive me crazy though. It's not real music

88

just tinkle-tinkle shit that sounds like breaking glass. It's good this place wasn't here back in the day. I would have been kicked out and 86'd.

Hey, there's Buffy. Thank God someone came in that I know. His hair is thin and grey, and he has put on some weight. His wife is with him and she's pushing a walker now. I'm going over to say hi. Talk to you later.

I'm back in my hotel room. Buffy's wife planted herself in front of her favorite slot machine and let her husband and I talk and drink for a few hours. He's happily retired now from the door plant but he had a lot of bad news, starting with Ott. When camp closed, our old hooker decided to use the education he received on the GI Bill and found a state job in the capital, which was good, but then he came down with diabetes and landed in a wheelchair. A few years later he died of a heart attack while driving to work. He was the first of many I heard about. According to Buffy, our co-workers were passing away from tragic diseases and car wrecks one after the other, and more of camp had disappeared than I thought.

My heart is aching from the news. No matter how much we complained about it, logging at Grisdale was in some ways the best times of our lives. At least it was for me because it keeps rewinding and playing back in my head, the good and the bad. While rehashing stories about Snow, Jed, Quiet Bob, Ott and several other men, I could tell it was still fresh in Buffy's head too. We both had questions that had never been answered.

"Did Quiet Bob fuck Lisa Rene or not?" he asked me. Rene had been the female lead in the movie Bob was in. Since then she had become a celebrity and was still making movies.

"No, for the millionth time. That's a myth, an urban legend. Rene didn't have anything to do with the likes of us. She was destined for stardom."

89

"That's what he said, too." Buffy sounded disappointed.

"Ruby asked me the same question. I didn't tell her Bob fucked some other actress who had a minor part. Bob told me that the last time he had sex with her they were on her bed going at it when he looked over his shoulder for some reason and saw two guys outside the bedroom window. One of them was pointing a video camera at them. The other guy was my cousin. He was giving the cameraman directions and apparently they were filming a movie candid camera style about a fresh young actor trying to make it in Hollywood. The actress Bob was on was helping them."

"Jeez, that may have been the beginning of reality TV."

"Maybe, but it didn't work out for them. Bob took sex seriously. He almost beat them up and threatened to quit the real movie."

"I'm glad he didn't. It was fun seeing him when it came out, even if he was wearing a football helmet. I've never known anyone else that was in a movie."

"I'm glad too. At least he made enough money to buy a truck and drive back up here. Otherwise, I probably would have had to go down there and get him. I have a question for you. Did Spike carry that knife around the first time he worked at Grisdale before he went to prison?"

"That fucking prick. Why did you have to remind me of him? No, to answer your question. Instead he told everybody he had a .44 Magnum in his rig and that they better be careful."

"That sounds about right. The knife must have been a prison thing. He called it his shank. I was surprised he let Bob touch it and taught him how to throw it."

"He was weird."

"That's for sure. He told Bob that he didn't believe it was possible for a man to rape his wife. I couldn't believe they became such good buddies. It made me sick. Larue even told

Bob how he had heard about Billy Gohl's buried treasure. An old jailbird in prison told him about it. We always wondered where Larue went in the evenings, and it turned out that Quiet Bob, true to his name, knew all along that Spike was looking for it with a metal detector, and didn't tell us." (Billy Gohl was a gangster in Aberdeen at the beginning of the last century. He started a merchant seamen's union and told sailors off sailing ships they could put their money in the union's safe while they were on shore. Then he killed them. He also had a trap door in the floor of his bar over the Wishkah River through which he shanghaied sailors to replace the ones he murdered. The authorities eventually put him in the insane asylum at Sedro Woolley where he died of old age. Nobody found the seamen's union fund until Larue came along.)

"You get to know everything about a man when you work in the brush with him," Buffy reminded me. "Didn't Larue teach him to throw an axe too?"

"No. Bob taught him. Bob had an uncle in Michigan who did lumberjack competitions. That's where he learned how to do it when he was a kid."

"I'm surprised Larue didn't stab Quiet Bob when he started fucking Ruby."

"I thought one of the big reasons why Ruby started fucking Bob was because he made her feel safe."

"I know. A lot of guys up there resented her. I couldn't believe some of the smack I heard. I always thought she was real sweet as well as good to look at."

"That's the truth."

"And if she hadn't stopped going out with him, she still might be alive.

"I hadn't thought of that." Actually I had. Many times.

"The lucky sucker. Every man in camp would have traded places with him, even the married ones like me. How many times do you think they screwed? A hundred? Two hundred? I'm glad I didn't live in camp and have to listen to it. It must have driven Spike crazy."

"It did me, at least for a while, but eventually they slowed down. Quiet Bob went over to the Sugar Shack every night after dinner. He told me that he couldn't stay away. That's when I knew the fool had fallen in love with her. After a month or so, Skoot told him he was starting to look like a spawned out salmon."

"Some guys were saying she broke up with him when he couldn't get it up any more."

"That could be true." But I knew it wasn't.

At the end of the evening, Buffy, without warning, started crying. "I never made a good engineer," he said. "I wanted to be good at it like Jed."

"What do you mean? You were a fine engineer. I worked under your rigging longer than anyone else. I never quit on you. I never told Crank I wouldn't work with you again. Jed, Skoot, and all the other donkey punchers were crazy assholes. They didn't mind taking risks with our lives. When they went ahead on a turn, they tried to push the yarders and rigging as far as possible. You weren't an asshole. The one time I got on your case to be more aggressive you nearly killed me."

"I'm surprised that you don't hate me for that. I was too meek."

"Come on. You weren't meek. If you were meek you never would have climbed into the cab and pulled back on the throttle. You were just gentle. Fuck! You were the only guy I know who could run the Triple Drum and that machine was a piece of shit. You pulled a lot of wood in with that rust bucket before they sent it to the scrap yard. Wasn't that fun?"

"Yeah, I admit it was. I could have been happy running the Triple Drum for a long time. Well, that's if they would have put some new glass in the windows for me so I could stay warm."

We laughed our butts off over that one. Before he went home, he asked me to come out to his car with him and his old lady to smoke some dope. I haven't been high in nearly 20 years and I'm still lit up. I may not get any sleep tonight.

"The Movie Star" was practically mobbed in the yard his first morning back. Crank even came out and told him he was going to be the second rigger on Tower 7. I couldn't believe it. The fucker quit, came back, and got the promotion I wanted, but what could I say? Crank knew I didn't like Larue. I watched Spike open the passenger door to the cab of 7's crummy, slide to the middle, and offer Bob the window seat. Like an idiot Bob rode out of camp sitting in the hooktender's spot rather than in back with the rest of the crew, not knowing he was being played.

I remember while getting a massage, before she and Bob started going out, I advised Ruby not to call him Cowboy Bob because he hated the name.

I remember he ignored her for a good month when he returned from Cali; then, during a weekend when Russ and I went to Bremerton for a wedding, he asked her to go to Aberdeen with him for a pizza. After that, he spent every evening in the "Sugar Shack" where she played him like a cat does a mouse until Thursday. I knew for a fact she gave it to him that night because he came in way after midnight, stumbled on a chair, got in his bunk and started snoring like a baby, the lucky bastard.

Larue became more discreet but he didn't stop harassing Ruby. One day after work, while plugging my whistles into the charger in the back of the office, I heard Spike talking to Ruby out front as he turned in his crew's time sheet.

"I told you, Spike. I don't want to go out with you."

"If I weren't an ex-con would you go out with me?"

93

"That's not it and you know it."

"You afraid of what the Cowboy would do? I'd sure hate to get him mad."

"Then don't."

"You two sure make a good looking couple. When you getting hitched?"

"Will you quit bugging me?"

I thought about leaving through the back door but cut through the building to the front door as usual and gave Larue a dirty look as I walked out.

I remember the morning I had a hard time crawling out of bed, and when I ran for the cookhouse before it closed found Ruby standing on the boardwalk between the cookhouse and office waiting for me. She was holding something in her arms and had on a silky print dress that didn't reach her knees. I couldn't help checking out her nylon clad legs.

"Ed, will you help me?"

"What do you want?"

"My high heel is stuck. Will you pull it out for me?"

I looked down her legs to her feet. One of her high heels was wedged in a crack between boards.

"If I take my foot out of my shoe I might snag my nylon on a sliver and get a run and I don't want to set this knitting down either."

I looked back up to the bundle of yarn she had clasped to her breasts.

"Is that what you do at work all day?" I asked as I set my own gear on the planks and kneeled.

"It's for my sister," she said. "I have to get it done before her wedding."

"Oh." I was used to being close to her but touching her feet, having my face so close to her legs, gave me a head rush. "Lift your foot."

For balance, she placed a hand on my head, sending a

jolt of electricity down my spine. Her ball of yarn fell to the planks and I grabbed it, wound it back up, and handed it to her after I pulled the heel of her shoe out of the crack.

"Thank you, Ed."

"You're welcome. Don't you think you should wear some other kind of shoes around here?"

"Don't you like the way these look?"

"They look okay but I don't think they are very practical are they?"

"I think they are very practical. I like them. Will you do one other thing for me Ed?"

"If you do something for me." I blurted that out unexpectedly, but I was worried that I wasn't going to have too many more opportunities to ask.

She looked disappointed.

"Don't worry," I told her. "It doesn't have anything to do with sex."

"I'm sorry but some of the men have been rude to me lately."

"So I've heard. What is it that you want?"

"Will you come in for a massage? You haven't let me give you one since I started seeing Bob. I need to talk to somebody and you are the only person at Grisdale I trust."

"OK. When? You two are with each other every night."

"This evening after dinner he is going to go look at elk tracks or something with Willy Slife. Can you meet me as soon as he leaves?

"Sure."

"What do you want?"

"I'll tell you then."

Ruby continued to the office and I hurried into the cookhouse calmer than before but was brought back to earth when I found only bread heels and gristle at the spike table.

"Shoe leather!" I yelped. "Nothing but old shoe leather

all the time."

"If you got up on time," Marg lectured me, "You wouldn't have this problem."

At that point in my career I had figured out it was best to ignore her. "This place is going to hell," I said more calmly. For breakfast Dodge gave me a cold pancake, cold bacon and cold fried eggs, which I folded into a sandwich and stuffed into my mouth as I jogged to the yard.

We didn't bother with the massage that night. She and I just sat in the front of the office with the shades down and talked.

"Is your love life getting you down?" I asked point blank, guessing that was the problem and not wanting to mess around. "At least you have one."

"How do you know? Has Bob said anything?"

"Are you kidding? Not him. But everybody else in camp is talking about you two, so it makes sense that you need to talk too."

"I do. I've made a mess of things. I don't think I can ever love again. I think it has died in me. But just looking at him stirred something in me. I don't know if it was love or lust or what but once he asked me out and we started to get to know each other, it erupted like a volcano and I couldn't help myself. He's so nice and kind. He's not like everyone else up here. Except for you of course. But now he has fallen in love with me and my feelings for him aren't as strong. I didn't think he would do that. I didn't want him to. I don't know what to do. I feel horrible."

"Lust and passion are good. And it's healthy to let them out. Don't persecute yourself."

"Thank you, Ed. Where did you learn that?"

"Not from experience. My mother is a shrink. I grew up listening to her talking to clients on the phone. Most of the time it was about love and sex."

"She probably makes a lot of money off people like me."

"Do you have a lot? Most of her clients are well off."

"And the rest of us suffer."

"So you don't love Bob. You are tired of him now. And you want to dump him. Don't worry about it. He's a big boy. He's probably broken someone else's heart, too."

I said that lightly and she smiled.

"Thanks. It's more complicated than that. Give me some credit."

"I give you lots of credit, Ruby. I think you are going to love again. The need and desire to love and be loved never dies. I heard my mom say that several times. I hope it's true. Why don't you give it a try with Bob? You might be surprised." I couldn't believe I was saying this stuff. It was coming out of my mouth as if I was channeling my mother. There's something I could spend a few bucks talking to a therapist about. I wouldn't return to this vein for decades.

"I can't, Ed. I just can't." She looked away for a moment at some other sad picture in her brain.

I didn't know what to say. A bunch of stuff was going through my head too, and I knew this conversation was getting out of my league. But my silence spurred her on. Quiet Bob must have known lots of secrets.

"There's more," she admitted. "A letter came from my husband the other day. It was sent to my old place and got lost in the mail for a while so I don't have much time. He's going to be home on vacation in a week and wants to see me. I can't say no, Ed. I know he doesn't always make me happy but he knows how to love me. Why can't Bob be happy and go to town with you and his other friends once in a while? When I'm with him I feel safe. This place scares me. Maybe I don't want to feel safe. What's wrong with me?"

She started balling so I put my arms around her. Her

sobs were deep and sharp and her body rubbed up and down against mine. My nose was in her hair and I breathed in her scent, sweetened lightly by perfume. It was easy to see why my friend had fallen in love with her and I got a dark vision of the rejection Quiet Bob was going to feel. Although the stupid choker dog between my legs grew as rigid as the stub of a broken limb, the rest of me tried to sway like a tree as I patted and rubbed her back.

After the tears quit flowing, she held on for a few moments then slowly eased away. "Thank you, Ed. You don't know how much your help means to me. I feel as if I have had the best from the best two men at camp. What do you want in return?"

So I pointed to the file cabinet and told her my sad story.

That made her cry again only this time not so wetly nor in a manner that required me to hug her.

"I don't have the keys to this one," she said as she pulled on the drawer. "I'll look for them but I imagine Turneau has a copy on his keychain. That might take a little while to get a hold of but I usually figure out how to get what I want." The wheels in her head were already turning. "If I can't, I'll just break in to it and blame it on someone else."

"You can blame it on me. Hell, just let me in some night. I bet I could knock that lock apart with a hammer and marlinspike in two seconds. They can't throw me in jail for finding out how my father died."

"Let me do it for you. I'm sure I'll get the key somehow. And don't worry, your secret is safe with me. I like secrets. I'm good with them."

I didn't realize it yet, but smiling and nodding my head in agreement when she said that, was like taking an oath with her that I would regret. She took most of the following week off, and before she left she told Bob she was going to Tacoma to see her girlfriend and to talk to an attorney about getting a divorce. So now I was helping her lie to my best friend, which didn't feel good. Oh well. I paid for it. He was a bear for the rest of the week and a total downer on the weekend. I agreed with Ruby. You would think going drinking with his buddies again would make him happy but wherever we went he sat and said absolutely nothing. Although he never told long stories, which was nice for those of us who liked to talk, his short comments, insights and jokes always rounded out the bullshit. His total silence and the brooding look on his face did the opposite.

When he got up to go to the can, Skoot, Greenbud, Glover and everyone else left. That left me alone with him. He just wanted to go back to camp, and since I was driving, I had to take him. Asking him what was wrong would have been stupid. I knew Ruby had flipped the disconnect switch and there was no way he couldn't feel the lack of current. She wasn't telling him the truth either and no way was I going to come clean and rat her out. Ruby could handle that one. I wasn't going to do her dirty work. He didn't want to do anything but wait in camp for her to come back. I sure in hell wasn't going to sit there with him so I took off and caught up with my friends.

Bob's truck was gone when I got back Sunday night. I walked over and saw that it wasn't at Ruby's either. Her car was there, though. A light was on and her window was wide open as it usually was. I went back to the bunkhouse. Bob finally came in after midnight. I heard his F-150 drive into the parking lot and shut down but he didn't turn the stereo off. He was listening to Willey Nelson's "Red-Headed Stranger," as if that was going to soothe his soul. I got out of bed, put my pants and slippers on, and walked out there. He was slumped sideways in his seat staring into the dark. When he had a lot to drink his pupils shrank and drew closer to his nose, and he was cross-eyed.

"Can you turn the music down?" I asked through the open window. "You're waking up camp."

"Fuck'm."

"What's the matter?"

"She kissed me off. She told me she didn't love me. She wouldn't even open the door when she got back. She told me she was going back to her husband."

"Why in the hell did she do that?"

"I don't know. I guess she likes him better than me. She told me she couldn't handle it anymore. She told me she was no good for me."

"Forget about her, Bob. Everybody saw it coming but you. And you can't really bitch about her going back to her husband."

"That's true."

He turned off the stereo and got out of his truck. We walked back to the hootch together and pissed from separate sides of the stairs before going inside. He crawled into his bunk with his clothes on.

Ruby didn't show herself in the cookhouse for a long time after that. I'm sure that was good for Bob. A few weeks later as I walked back from the yard at the end of the day, Turneau came out and asked me if I had looked in my mailbox lately. My mailbox was a cubbyhole with a "K" above it in an array of 24 boxes on the wall next to the office door, and every once in a while I glanced at mine. A big manila envelope was sitting there now and Turneau told me that it had been there a few days. I pulled it out and immediately knew what it was. I didn't recognize the handwriting, and the return address was that of "A Secret Admirer." It was postmarked from Tacoma, and on the flap in back "Please Open When Alone" was written in small letters. To top it off it smelled like perfume.

I smiled and told Turneau thanks. He hadn't gone back inside and was watching me look at the envelope.

"I'm dying of curiosity, Knucklehead. Aren't you going to give me a clue about who that is from?"

Ruby probably had been listening to him speculate about the contents since it arrived.

"No," I told him and walked away.

Too much was going on at the bunkhouse to open the package there. After eating dinner I took it to my truck and drove to the dam. With the panorama of the lake and the two ridgelines of the hills where we worked before me, I sliced open the envelope with my pocketknife and pulled out the contents. The entire file was inside. My father's name, Floyd Cranbrook, was typed on the tab, along with the date of his death, Sept. 22, 1953. Before I opened it up, I read the note she had written on a separate piece of paper and scotch taped to the front of the file.

"Ed, someday when things settle down, I'll tell you how I got a hold of this. It's really funny and I'm sure it will make you laugh. I hope it is what you want. I didn't think it would be right to look at it until after you did. Honest. Your friend, Ruby. P.S. Let me know if you want to talk."

I opened the folder. The sides were stiff and I doubt if it had been looked at in 25 years. I still have it by the way. Only a two page carbon copy of the accident report was inside. "For original copy and complete file, see Central Filing at Shelton Office" was typed in red letters across the top. The top half of the first sheet was filled with standard information: name, home address, date of birth, date of accident, location of accident, next of kin (my grandparents Angus and Molly whom I don't remember meeting) and so on. Nothing grabbed my attention until I came to employee's position. There it said "chokerman" and beside that was "the deceased was working out-of-class as a third rigger at time

101

of accident."

Under "Description of Accident" it read as follows: "Floyd Cranbrook was killed while topping a Douglas Fir tailtree at an elevation approximately 50 feet above the ground. The tree was sound, approximately three feet in diameter at the base, and nearly two and one-half feet in diameter at the location where he was topping it. While ascending the tree using standard climbing gear, Mr. Cranbrook sawed off several limbs without incident and given instructions where to top the tree by his supervisor, Wilbur Johansen, who was standing on the ground. Mr. Cranbrook proceeded to undercut the top of the tree with his saw. The wedge fell out in one piece. Mr. Cranbrook then began to make the back cut with the saw. All appeared normal until the top began to tip. At that time Mr. Johansen and a second man on the ground, Darin Jackson, claim to have seen the tree top begin to pull wood and slab. As the slab of wood began to peel down the tree, it pulled Mr. Cranbrook's climbing rope tight which squeezed him next to the tree and most likely rendered him incapable of taking any action to save his life. Then the slab of wood broke Mr. Cranbrook's climbing rope as the slab with the treetop still attached separated and fell from the trunk of the tree. Mr. Cranbrook plummeted to the ground and landed head first, breaking his neck. Both Johansen and Jackson reported that the logger's neck was disjointed to such a degree that they judged he had already expired and that any effort to revive him would be unsuccessful. The county coroner agreed and noted in his autopsy report that extensive injuries to the victim's pelvis and lower back from being pulled against the tree and to his skull upon impact with the ground were also severe enough to cause death."

Crank and Sprint were listed as the only witnesses. They had also signed the report along with the man I assumed to be the camp superintendent at the time, Crank's father.

Below the description was a hand drawn diagram showing the tail tree, its proximity to the road and orientation to the logging show it was part of, and the location of my father's body. The yarder had not yet been brought in and Crank, Sprint and my father were in the process of getting the show ready for the yarding crew to arrive and start work. A few days before that they had stood up and rigged the spar tree with the help of a larger crew.

After reading the report, I put it back into the file and the file back into the envelope. I sat there for a while wondering if I should take the report at face value or attempt to get more information from the two men who were there, and from my mother. I knew I was going to ask questions. Something about the report didn't add up. Crank had made his mark as a climber and as the head of the rig-up crew when he was a young man. Sprint also had a reputation for being a top-notch climber. I had never topped and rigged a tree. However, I remembered Ott prepping Snow before sending Snow up to top one. I distinctly recall him telling Snow to cut the corners before making his back cut. Cutting the corners meant sawing into both sides of the tree a few inches parallel to the direction you wanted it to fall because every once in a while the tree or the tree top in this case would begin tipping before the back cut got close to the undercut, and start to peel wood fiber on the side of the tree as it hinged over. On a tree being sawed down at ground level, that wasn't a problem but when a man was strapped around a tree high in the air, that was a big problem. Cutting the corners decreased the chances of that happening. Did Crank tell my dad to cut the corners? Why was he even up in the tree? Both Crank and Sprint were paid a lot more money for doing that work. Third riggers got a few cents more per hour than a chokerman to work as pack horses for climbers and pull rigging up to them on the passline.

By the way, Snow climbed down the tree he topped and said he never needed to do that again. Bob, on the other hand, strapped on the spurs and belt whenever possible. I never had much of a desire to climb. Go figure.

10.

Day 5, on the way to the sheriff's office.

It's ten to eight in the morning. I've had breakfast. Thanks to the hotel, my clothes are clean. I am checked out and sitting in the casino parking lot about to drive to the Sheriff's office, 25 miles from here. The meeting is at 10.

Buffy's wife didn't seem happy to see me last night. I don't blame her. I imagine her husband used to go home and complain about me yelling at him, and I appreciate how she left the two of us alone to talk about the good old days.

While drinking beers with him, a few of his friends came over to our table and said hello. They had worked at Grisdale too and recognized me but I have to admit I only remembered the one named Rick Halitos. You can imagine what we called him. He was a truck driver Quiet Bob had saved one day. Bob was driving the crummy from the tailend to the landing when he rounded a corner and found Rick's truck parked in a wide spot with smoke billowing out the window. Halitos had fallen asleep and dropped his cigarette into the greasy rags and garbage on the floor. Bob opened the door, pulled out Comatose, which was one of his nicer nicknames, grabbed the fire extinguisher and put the fire out before much damage was done. A few moments later, Rick would have been Comatoast.

Rick, the other guys, and Buffy for that matter, were men we looked down our noses at. I confess that being highballers gave us superiority complexes. The more wood we logged the better we felt about ourselves. There was another group of men that didn't need that stimulus. Buffy fell into that crowd. He swung between us and the group who had nothing good to say about their jobs with the company. Crank would have fired every last one of them if it weren't for the union. After a successful grievance where the company was forced to hire someone back that Crank had sent down the road for something stupid, that person became untouchable. As long as he showed up to work sober and on time everyday and went through the motions for eight hours, anything Crank did to him after that was harassment. I always wondered why those guys even showed up for work. Crank was never going to promote them. They didn't act like they wanted one. Some of them knew the union contract forward and backwards, attended all the meetings in Shelton, and made it clear that they were not going to do anything more than was necessary.

When I asked Quiet Bob why he didn't rat out Halitos to Crank or Hunt, Bob said that he didn't think Rick was a bad guy and that the truck driver was struggling to survive like everyone else. Besides, he wanted to hear the excuse Halitos was going to give the truck foreman for the charred upholstery.

I didn't have as much compassion as my friend did. In order for me to be civil to Rick and his friends last night, I had to imagine they had at one time paid their dues on a rigging crew and earned the right to call themselves loggers. The other reason I didn't lapse into my old self was because after listening to the stories about our ex-coworkers who had died early, I realized that Rick and friends deserved credit for still breathing. They were part of the landscape I had been looking at the past few days and were like the trees that hadn't been planted by humans growing between the stumps. I remember watching yew trees under the cables spring back up every time we yarded logs over them, turn after turn all day long. They were attached to the land someway I never would be.

The best Crank and his siderods could do was try and build crews out of men who got along with one another and had similar work ethics. Putting a highballing rigging slinger on the crew run by a hooktender who no longer was driven to get as many loads out as possible was as bad of an idea as putting a competent yet laid back slinger on the crew run by a log hungry sonofabitch. Crank probably thought it was a good year when he had six or eight average crews he could count on for five loads a day and one or two crews who got ten or more.

Bob was a good fit on Spike's crew according to the above criteria but I figured they would eventually turn on one another. Spike wanted men that he could intimidate and manipulate. That wasn't going to work with Bob. My friend believed that he had to show others what he wanted in order to get it out of them and it was only a matter of time before Spike picked on someone that Bob would protect. Spike though was smart enough not to let that happen. Towards the end of summer the hooktender on Tower 20 quit and Spike talked Crank into giving the job to Quiet Bob.

That was hard for me to watch. I could still see Snow handing Bob the extra whistle, and Tower 20 was the best yarder in camp, if not on the entire Olympic Peninsula. It was a large, powerful, slackline machine built by Washington Iron Works. The only negative was that it was stationed in the Canyou River drainage east of the Wynoochee. That was probably why Spike hadn't taken the job for himself. The company had another reload over there plus it served as a staging point for four crews. There was no office, so it was administered out of Grisdale and fell under Crank's domain. He joked about Canyou River but recently had appointed Hunt to be the new siderod over there, which was good.

Another thing going for him was that King Douglas was his rigging slinger and Tommy Trailhead his second rigger. Quiet Bob had stump broke both of them when they were fresh out of high school and wanted to prove they were tough enough to be loggers. Both had been good athletes in school and with them Slacker 1's load count surged way ahead of all the other crews for a season. They were party animals too and liked to chase the hometown girls so the previous year they had taken the opportunity to transfer to Canyou River because it was closer to town and they could get some sleep while riding the bus. Bob had to get up thirty minutes early to catch the crummy the company sent over there every day for the few men who lived in Grisdale. He got back late too, so the cookhouse was practically empty when he came in. With Trailhead and King on his crew I knew they were going to kick ass. By then I was used to the fact that Quiet Bob would always be promoted before me, so on his first day I waited until he got back to eat dinner. I expected him to be as high as a kite but instead he looked as if his dog had been hit by a car.

"Not good," Bob replied when I asked him how it had gone.

"Oh yeah? What happened? Pull a tailhold?"

"I wish. I got in a pissing match with the yarder engineer."

It was a common story. The yarder engineer, who everyone called Vulture because he drew cartoons in which the loggers were vultures and crows, quit listening to the whistles as soon as King blew for him to go ahead on a turn. There wasn't a yarder engineer in the world who thought they needed the slinger's instructions about what cable to pull on, and they were probably right most of the time, but the slinger could see the wood and the rigging and what was happening in the brush and the engineer couldn't most of the time. He could only feel it by how the waves of tension traveled up the cables and shook the yarder and how the engine changed octaves as it pulled. Although it was everybody's concern, getting the logs safely to the landing was King's primary responsibility and as boss of the entire operation, Quiet Bob knew that if a cable did break and kill someone while a turn was being yarded in and he had to say that the reason why that man was injured was because the engineer didn't heed the slinger's whistles and had been getting away with doing so for some time, it would be his, the hooktender's, fault. No way was Quiet Bob going to let that happen. He had trained King how to pull rigging so as soon as he saw what was happening, Bob stopped everything and went up to the landing to talk to Vulture.

They started yelling at each other almost as soon as he got there and didn't stop until Bob got on the radio and asked Hunt to drive up to the show.

Hunt listened to them. He knew Bob would quit if he didn't support the new hooktender. He also knew that skilled slackline yarder engineers were harder to replace than hooktenders so in some ways the engineer was more valuable. On the other hand, Vulture had a family and lived in the village because it was cheap and he was in debt. He couldn't just pack up and go somewhere else. He couldn't quit. Life had him by the balls and Hunt only sighed deeply and with a frown on his old face told Vulture he better start paying attention to the whistles and doing what they said. Crank would have smiled while saying that.

Vulture didn't have to hear an ultimatum. "OK," he said. "I'll follow whatever god-damned whistle the slinger blows in." Bob started to talk but Vulture cut him off. "I don't need you to tell me how to do my fucking job," he snarled as he climbed the ladder back up to the cab and slammed the door.

"So why does that make you feel bad?" I asked Bob. "It would make me feel good."

"Because I don't know if I like having that much power over men's lives. Now I know why Snow told Crank that he didn't want to be a hooktender."

"Don't worry about it, brother. I sure wouldn't," I boasted without a clue of what I was talking about. "Kick butt and take names later. It's part of the job. Maybe you just saved someone's life and will never know it."

Quiet Bob liked that last part. "Thanks," he said.

The logs began flowing to the landing after that. They finished the show in a couple of weeks and moved Tower 20 to a new claim full of big wood. We called those pumpkin patches. Ten loads a day was a piece of cake. Seeing how they were going to be sitting on that landing until the snow flew, Tower 20 had a chance of getting more wood than any other machine that year.

Spike boasted Tower 7 became the most productive crew the day he took it over, and he wagered a bottle of whiskey with Quiet Bob over who would win the title. Other men bet money and the daily load counts for each machine became common knowledge. Nobody took it that seriously though. It was just entertainment and something amusing to watch as the weather turned wet and cold. It wasn't until Crank put Red Bodene on Tower 20 that the competition became more intense.

Red was another young gun from Shelton. He had gone to school with Trailhead and King and had followed them to Grisdale a couple of years after they started setting chokers. He wanted to be a logger just as much as anyone but about the time he began working in the woods he started going out with Crank's daughter, which wasn't a good career move. I remember him coming by Crank's "cattle ranch" in early July when we were there helping our boss with his haying. Every year Crank conned a bunch of us into spending a long Saturday busting ass throwing bales of hay onto a truck then off loading them into his barn. We usually had a good time. His wife cooked us breakfast, lunch and dinner and when we were done, Crank got us drunk. Late in the afternoon that year when we were almost done and had stopped for our first beer, Bodene drove up the long driveway in a loud Mustang and nearly shit when he got out of the car and saw most of Grisdale's top loggers there to greet him.

Crank got that tight-lipped smile on his face that we all had learned to read as a warning sign, but luckily Maggie came out of the house and saved Red. She had been driving the flatbed truck all day but in about twenty minutes had showered and made herself look so good we all felt stupid for thinking she was a tomboy. She was home from college for the summer and 21. I can't imagine her father had any say about who she went out with. Crank took great pride in being a logger but it was obvious it galled him that she was having a summer romance with a chokerman. That he waited until September after his girl went back to school to do anything about it seemed a little weak to me. By then the two kids had agreed to break up. That didn't stop Crank from transferring Red to Spike's crew and telling his most sadistic hooktender to fire the man.

For most green men, having the boss unleash his dog on you would be the beginning of the end, but Bodene was no pussy. Unbeknownst to Spike, Red didn't live in the bunkhouses because every night after he got back to town he went to a boxing gym and worked out. Although he was skinny and only weighed 185 pounds at the time, his dream was to be a true heavyweight. You would think Crank might have known that, but he probably thought everything his daughter told him about Red was bullshit, which it wasn't. Whatever the case, he didn't warn Larue how the budding heavyweight might know how to take care of himself.

According to Russ, who had taken Bob's place on the crew, Spike went into the rigging and got into Bodene's face. Yelling at him to go faster and work harder didn't do any good because he was already working as hard and as well as the other two chokermen, and he seemed to have the ability to tune Spike out. Spike started telling him to choke one log then screamed at him for choking the wrong log. When Bodene started unbelling the log, Spike lit into him for slowing down the crew. Spike went at him like that for a couple of days then finally came up with the idea of sending him up to the landing for a skyhook. The landing was a twenty-minute climb up hill.

"There's no such thing as a skyhook," Red told Spike.

"What do you mean? Do I look like a fucking idiot? I've been logging for as long as you've been alive."

Red just looked at him and raised his eyebrows. "The guys on Tower 6 already played that trick on me. What kind of fucking idiot do you think I am?"

"You think I don't know what I'm talking about? Those women on 6 don't know shit about logging. Get your ass up to the landing and get a skyhook I'm telling you or I'm firing your ass."

"Go ahead if that's what you want to do. Go get a skyhook yourself."

"You're fired. Get the fuck out of here."

"What am I fired for?" Bodene laughed. "For refusing to get a skyhook? The union will have a field day with that one."

"For insubordination you motherfucker!" Spike picked

up a piece of a limb and cocked it back as if he was going to club Red with it. "I told you to leave now you fucking piece of shit!"

Red stepped towards Larue quickly, ducked around Spike as he swung the club, then grabbed it out of Spike's hand. He poked Spike in the chest with it and Spike fell on his butt. He came up in a flash with his knife in his hand.

"Go ahead asshole. You make one step towards me with that blade and I'll bust you up so bad the crew will have to pack you out."

That's when Russ jumped between them and told them to knock it off. Russ had good timing when it came to stopping fights. He turned his back on Spike and told Red to leave and catch a logging truck to camp.

"I will," Red said, "but nobody better say I quit." With that he stalked off.

Red didn't come to work the next day. Instead, he called the office and told Turneau he was going into the union to file a grievance and talk to the business rep. I think it was one of the few times I saw a man use the union for what it was supposed to be used for, but then Red's father worked at one of the mills so he was getting some good counseling. A lot of phone calls were made that day. Russ was summoned to the office after work to describe what he had seen to the shop steward and Crank. There were more phone calls and Red was told that if he still wanted a job to show up at Canyou River instead of Grisdale the next day, which was fine with him because the bus ride was a lot shorter. Better yet, when he got there, he found out he was being put on a crew with two of his friends and old football teammates.

Crank showed up at Canyou River too that morning, which he did once a week. Before the crews left, he took Bob off to the side and told him to fire Bodene, that he was a troublemaker. When Bob went out in the rigging to work with

Bodene that day he saw right away that the kid was working his ass off. He couldn't fire Red. Crank drove over a couple of days later to find out why Bodene was still around. "He's a good hand," Bob told him. "There's no reason to run him off. The crew is better with him on it." Crank turned red but didn't say anything and drove away. Bob told me he knew that he would be on Crank's shit list from then on. But so were a lot of other good men at Grisdale, he added. Besides, he liked being one of Hunt's boys over at Canyou River. Crank had been telling us for years that the men who worked at Canyou River were culls. Bob said he was going to enjoy watching Crank eat those words at the end of the season when Tower 20 out produced everyone else. What really made this amusing to me though was that shortly thereafter I got my first hooking job and was sent over to Canyon River, too. In fact, I became somewhat of a technical problem for Bob to work out in order for him to reach his goal.

When cutting timber on Tower 20's new show, the fallers uncovered a knoll the timber cruisers and logging engineers had missed. It stuck up high enough that Tower 20 was not going to be able to reach over the top of it with its skyline and yard the logs on the far side. Thus the guys in the office had a cat road built down to the top of the knoll and a landing scraped on the top big enough for the Triple Drum to sit. The Triple Drum was an old Caterpillar D-8 bulldozer converted into a small yarder that was used to log units too small for full-sized machines and corners of larger shows like this one that couldn't be reached any other way. Since logging trucks couldn't get up and down the steep cat road, the Triple Drum was going to pull the logs up from the far side of the knoll and a bulldozer was going to push the logs over the side that Tower 20 could reach. Having to choke and yard each log twice was expensive, but when pulling logs out of the cold deck, 20 was going to get 20 loads a day easy. Spike complained so loud that Crank placated his favorite asshole by saying Tower 20 would only get credit for half those loads. However, ultimately, it wasn't up to him to decide but to the managers and bean counters in town that put together the production reports they were using as scorecards. Crank assured Spike he would talk to Big Boy, the boss in Shelton, about it.

Anyway, getting back to the Triple Drum; it hadn't been used for a while so Crank had to form a new crew and he asked me if I wanted to be the hooker. I didn't exactly jump at the chance for it was one more dirty job he wanted me to do, but I said okay. I'd get a pay raise, and when I was done with swinging logs for 20, he had a real unit for me to log. That sounded good. "I hate to send you over to Canyou River, though, Knucklehead," he lamented to me. "There's something about that place that ruins every good man I send there. See that it doesn't happen to you."

I had more immediate problems. One. The Triple Drum was a bundle of worn out metal parts. It had a mainline drum, a haulback drum and a haywire drum and could actually pull in a decent turn when the frictions and hydraulics were working, but I swear every section of haywire on that piece of crap was rotten and I don't know how many times I broke it during road changes. That pissed the hell out of me. Another thing was that it was puny compared to Tower 20. The tower on it was only 80-feet tall compared to 20's 120-foot tube. How's that for Freudian symbolism? It looked small sitting down in the middle of the unit. To add insult to injury, we had to walk down the cat road a quarter-mile to get to our show. Thus we couldn't even eat lunch in the crummy on a rainy day. At night the cat operator let us pile on the bulldozer and carried us up the hill to the road. That was as good as it got. To top it off, Crank assigned Buffy to be my engineer.

Poor Buffy hadn't panned out on any of the big

machines and this was his last chance to run yarder. At first I thought that was going to be our downfall, but after we got going it turned out his sense of humor and optimism were what I needed. My responsibilities were a lot tougher to get used to than I thought they would be, even on the Triple Drum. But it was my first hooktending job and I could still hear Jed's words, "Show the bastards you can handle it."

I'm in Montesano now, in the parking lot at the Sheriff's office waiting to go in to see the homicide detective. It's time to get serious. Ruby. She was the one who was doomed, not me.

Spike was doomed too. He cut his own throat. With Quiet Bob out of the picture for most of the day, Spike started harassing Ruby again whenever he saw her so she resumed eating with my friends and me. In that regard a sense of normalcy developed that would last pretty much until the end of the season. However there was nothing normal about Spike or Ruby.

In September, in the cookhouse in front of everybody but Quiet Bob, Spike asked her real loud if she could be the prize for getting the most wood.

"Will you grow up Spike and leave me alone? I'm tired of you harassing me."

"If you don't like it then don't come in here when I'm eating. You'd be doing us both a favor. But you can't do that can you because if you come in earlier than me in the morning and later than me in the evening then you'll be here when Cowboy Bob is eating. I don't see why he gets special treatment. It breaks my heart every time I see you. I'd say you've got a problem."

"No, you do!" she nearly screamed and walked out.

All the guys but me laughed. Dodge, Bee and Marge

didn't think it was funny either, and in the cookhouse their opinions mattered. Dodge told Crank that if Spike didn't apologize to Ruby he'd quit feeding Spike. Camp cooks had a lot of sway if the men liked their food. It wasn't that we loved his cooking but we were so used to it that we complained when he tried altering the menu. Sirloin Steak on Monday, Seafood on Tuesday, Prime Rib on Wednesday, and T-bones on Thursday. Crank knew that he could find a new cook that would feed us the same meat, but there was only a 50-percent chance that we'd want to eat it the way he or she prepared it. And if we didn't want to eat it, then Crank might have to fill a lot more vacancies, which wasn't a problem he wanted to confront towards the end of the season when the question of whether or not he'd get his quota was still in the balance. He knew that most of the homeguards in the village, the men who rode the town buses and most of the men in the bunkhouses hated Spike's guts. That's why he liked Spike so much, because Spike was spit in their faces, but he couldn't afford a mutiny that time of year.

The next day, according to Russ, Crank drove to their unit and told the hooktender he had to apologize to Ruby. Spike fumed about it for the rest of the day, but when the crummy got back to camp that night, he went straight to the office and in front of everyone who could hear said he was sorry "for being so insensitive and persistent about teasing" her and that the only reason he had acted that way was because she was "so pretty I didn't know how to express my feelings for you any other way."

Ruby told me later on that night when I went over for a massage that she took the opportunity to say in front of everyone that she was sorry his disappointment had made him act so childishly, but that she was thankful he would no longer be speaking to her except about business. She told me that she was afraid of Spike. "Why do you stay here? Why don't you quit?" I asked her. "Because I don't have a place to go until my husband gets home, and because I told them I'd stay for the entire season," she answered. "Besides, I'm not going to let that asshole run me out of camp. I have made some friends here like you and leaving is going to make me sad."

I didn't know what to say to that. "It's a good thing Crank's on your side."

"Crank?" she laughed. "He's the worst of them all. He doesn't care a thing about me. He groped me a couple of times after I first started working here. He's the only one who has gone that far."

"No shit?"

"No shit. I hate it when men do that. Why are most men stupid pigs? Why can't guys learn that it's the ones who are polite that get the rewards, like you and Bob?"

"It hasn't gotten me much."

"It hasn't? What about these massages? You are the only person in camp I give them to. Have you ever told Bob?"

"No. Are you kidding?"

"That's good. I never gave him one. I saved them just for you."

"Ruby, I have to confess," I laughed. "My thoughts about you aren't so pure."

"As if I don't know? I like playing with fire." She patted me on the belly. "That's it for tonight though."

And one last thing before I go in. In October, Bob received a telegram from Snow. "In trouble. Please wire airfare to A Express Acapulco." That amounted to a chunk of change for loggers and I pitched in more than half of it. A few days later Bob and I drove over to SeaTac Airport to pick him up. We were anxious to see our old friend and hear his story. It was sure to be about a run-in with the law or drug lords and involve wild sex with beautiful women, but when we saw him stagger off the plane, we both realized the ride back to Shelton and camp was going to be disappointing.

He had lost at least 20 pounds and looked like hell. He could barely walk straight. The first words out of his mouth were, "Man, you wouldn't believe the amount of coke I snorted. It was cheap and pure. I spent every fucking dime I had on it. Take me to Pierre's will you? I have to come down. I feel like shit. Thanks for rescuing me, brothers."

Snot was practically dripping out of his nose and he snuffed every ten seconds. His speech had a nasal quality to it and he had developed a lisp. He was still dressed in dirty shorts and sandals and his old sea bag was so empty it looked like a deflated beach ball. When he took off his sunglasses, we saw that his eyes were sunken and bloodshot. When he got on the plane, they were probably bugging out of his head. Back then a person would have been able to stretch out a few thousand bucks for eight months in Mexico and Central America but not if he or she were doing good coke. There was more to the story, but we were going to have to be patient to hear it.

He showed up at camp a week later looking for work. For him to come back and ask Crank for a job had to have been humiliating. Crank always crowed when somebody he had had a fight with returned and groveled. Watching Snow do it was embarrassing and I wish our friend had poked his head in the office and told Crank to fuck off one more time. But that wasn't the case. He looked better but it was obvious he wasn't fit for the brush yet. Crank offered him the chaser's job on my new crew and acted like he was doing the world a favor. Snow didn't hesitate to take it. He should have been going into a rehab center instead but in those days nobody thought cocaine was addictive. He was going to have to tough it out with us in the bunkhouses. I told Buffy to be careful with him on the landing. Like everyone else, Buffy loved Snow and mothered him through those first couple of weeks.

I'm going into the office. I thought about leaving the recorder on and putting it in my pocket but have decided not to because I don't know what they would do if they discovered I had wired myself. I don't want to lose what I have already said about this story so I am turning it off and leaving it on the seat. Will report back when I come out.

11.

Day 5, recorded in the parking lot after talking to the homicide detective.

The deputy told me to take a seat when I checked in, so I took a few steps backwards and stood with my arms crossed. A few moments later Loraine Goodwell came out. I figured she had moved on or retired so was surprised to see her. When she questioned me 25 years ago, she looked 10 years older than me. Now she looked younger and I don't think she was dying her hair. She was also showing a little cleavage through a slightly opened blouse under her coat not like the first time I met her when she was buttoned all the way to her neck. I hoped she wasn't still a bitch, though. J.T. Brown had told me to try not to get upset with her back then, that she was a token at that time, a young woman being given a chance to make it as a female detective in a county with lots of secrets buried in in the woods because it wasn't expected that she would succeed, and she knew it.

"A pleasure to see you, Mr. Knockle. Thank you for coming in," she extended her hand to me.

"You too. Congratulations for lasting so long." I said without thinking.

"What do you mean?"

"Years ago when I first met you, my attorney told me you were being set up to fail. It's obvious that didn't happen."

"Thank you," she smiled. "I had to be tough. I still do although I hope I have finally learned how to make use of my natural charm. It appears you have, unless you turned into a con man. Please come on back."

She led me into her office. From the photos of her standing alongside politicians and the framed certificates on the wall, it was obvious she had done more than keep her job.

"This will only take a moment," she said as she reached for a plastic lab bag on her desk, opened it up, and pulled out a small cotton ball on the end of a plastic stick. "Just open your mouth wide and let me swab the inside of your cheek. You can do it yourself if you want."

"Go ahead." I opened wide.

A few seconds later she zip locked my mucus into the lab bag.

"That's it?" I asked her when she was done. "That's what I traveled all the way from Argentina for?"

"It is."

"I'm glad I didn't have to pay for the plane ticket."

"We could water board you if you are looking for more excitement, or pull out the thumb screws, but your attorney has become famous and he is still in practice. I know you would want to call him. Over the years he and I have worked the opposite sides of a few other cases and I have to admit Mr. Brown helped me become a better cop."

"That's nice. He's as curious as I am about why you want my DNA?"

"Simple. We gathered many pieces of evidence that we couldn't analyze back then. Now, thanks to advances in science, we have better tools and before I retire, I want to sort out what happened. That was my first murder case. It was never solved beyond a shadow of a doubt in my opinion."

"You don't think Spike Larue killed her?"

She didn't answer and, instead, looked at me intensely before she spoke. "My instincts tell me you are not the person who murdered the beautiful secretary at Grisdale, but my experience with other innocent witnesses who hire attorneys to make sure their rights are protected during investigations tells me you know something that you don't want me to find out. On a more personal level and as a woman, I cannot fathom why or how Ruby Faulk ever wanted to interject herself into a place like Grisdale among a bunch of filthy low-life loggers."

Years ago I would have exploded. Instead, I laughed and said, "I have often wondered the same thing."

"Well done, Mr. Knockle. I can see why you didn't bring Mr. Brown with you this time."

"Who knows? Perhaps after analyzing my DNA you'll want to call me back in, at which time I'd be happy to comply as long as you pay for the plane ticket again. And maybe I'll bring Mr. Brown with me."

"I'd enjoy that."

"Besides, I have to admit that I am curious about what my DNA will tell you."

"And what could that be?" She tried to sound casual and friendly as if she were joking because she knew I would not tell her anything, but I like to think I heard her voice catch then speed up slightly like a chainsaw sometimes does before it runs out of gas.

"I'm sorry. I'm sure that if my worst fears come true, you'll tell me."

This time her laughter sounded real.

"Mr. Knockle, you play this game very well now."

"I'm an innocent man. Plus I have a great attorney."

"He is good at making my job difficult."

With that the interview ended.

Although I probably looked confident, I was having a panic attack as I walked out. While talking to her, the question arose in my head about what I would do if my DNA showed that Crank was my father? That was so fucking ridiculous that the idea made me laugh like a maniac and loud enough for them to hear me in the building.

Back in the truck before turning on the recorder, I let the paranoid freak calm down. I knew what my DNA would reveal. J.T. assured me a long time ago it had no consequence and told me not to worry about it. But sometimes I can't even follow my own advice.

Ruby was going to quit working at Grisdale on the last day of November and rejoin her husband. About two weeks before then, I went up to the office for my final massage. She started on my back as usual then had me roll over so she could massage my front. She started on my face and head then worked down my neck through my shoulders and arms then back to my chest. Normally she stopped there but this time her hands moved down my belly.

"This is something new."

"Since this is probably going to be our last time . . . you don't mind do you?" she said and smiled.

I couldn't stop her from working down past my belly. I didn't want to live up to my nickname. Nor could I stop myself from kissing and touching her or from pulling her onto the counter with me. That's where we did it, right there on the counter where every logger who had ever worked at Grisdale had done their business with the company. I also have to admit that although I wasn't a virgin, I had never fucked a woman who wasn't drunk and unsure of herself or wondering why she was having sex with me. Ruby was the first woman

I ever made love with who knew what she wanted and how to enjoy it.

Five minutes after we were done, nobody would have guessed we had just had sex. We hugged and kissed a little bit and said nice things to one another but as I left I couldn't help wonder if it was little more than a handshake goodbye. I had heard the rumors that other men had been fucking her behind Quiet Bob's back, and now I was another one. I felt like shit all of a sudden.

I imagine my load trickled out of her and into her panties as she walked back to her hootch that night. When she got ready for bed, she took them off and threw them into an empty clothes hamper. Unfortunately, she never had to do her laundry again. I figured the cops took her dirty clothes back to town and found all sorts of stains and dried globs of bodily fluid they could not link to sources. I figured Loraine Goodwell must have saved some of the samples and in a few weeks was going to find out that I had done it with Ruby, along with the names of some of the other men in camp who were boinking her, too. I don't know what Goodwell was going to do with that information. My attorney told me it was fairly useless as far as I was concerned and did more harm to Ruby's reputation than to mine. But I hadn't been sure about that. I knew I didn't want Bob to find out because I didn't have the guts to tell him myself.

12.

Day 5 and 6, back in camp.

I bought as many cans of beer as my cooler could hold, drove back to camp and am now sitting on the ice chest under the tree again next to a fire I laid but haven't lit. I've already written a note explaining that the stash of beer is for other ex-residents of Grisdale who come here. I don't imagine it will last long no matter who finds it, but at least I will get to drink a few cans while they are cold. I also have the uneaten half of a large pizza, some energy bars, a bottle of coke and some cold coffee. The rain has stopped. The sun is out and a lot of daylight is left. I'm going to sit here and finish the story even if it takes me all night. Tomorrow, I catch a red eye to Atlanta, then fly to South America. Here it goes.

In November, 1979, I called Mama knowing she would ask me to come to the family mansion in Seattle for Thanksgiving dinner. I always turned her down, so accepting the invitation that year was a big surprise. I told her I wanted to bring a friend then asked Quiet Bob to go.

I would finally have to tell him who I was, and looking back, I wonder if the reason I wanted to was because I had dipped into Ruby's reservoir of love. I had other motives, too. Crank was being a dipshit. Ever since Bob had refused to fire Bodene, Crank took every opportunity to screw Tower 20. Spike and his boys worked overtime whenever they wanted to. Bob's crew couldn't get any. The mechanics went to Spike's show first thing every evening to service Tower 7 but Bob had to wait until Tower 20 was about to quit running before he could get anything fixed. That was normal bullshit though for crews in Canyou River, and despite his lack of support, Bob's side kept getting more wood than Spike's, which was enough to keep Bob from complaining. I wouldn't have been able to stay silent though, especially the Monday morning he got to work and found someone had topped two tailtrees on his show over the weekend.

Quiet Bob had been looking forward to doing that himself. A rigging man couldn't consider himself to be an all around logger until he was an experienced climber. Hunt figured Bob might quit when he saw that someone else had done his work. It was a big insult, and the siderod followed the crummy to the landing to prevent him from tramping. Bob did get hot, especially after Hunt told him that Spike had baited Crank by telling him he didn't think Crank could climb anymore. Not that it took much to get Crank to exercise his ego. Spike knew what he was doing.

Hunt told me later that Bob's eyes glowed like the Devil's. Bob told Snow and me that when he got to work and saw the trees, it felt as if someone had reached into his pants and jacked him off while he was passed out in a bar. Snow suggested that he pretend it had been a woman because they had actually done him a favor. Hell, Bob could have filed a grievance with the union, but he didn't.

The tailtrees were for holding the skyline over the cold deck of logs the Triple Drum had yarded off the far side of the knoll. Bob and Trailhead rigged the trees and when they started using them a few days later, it was easy picking for the rigging crew. They averaged 25 loads a day for the week before Thanksgiving. That was an entire trainload of logs and whether or not to credit them to Tower 20 had already become a hot topic. Crank told me that he thought the Triple Drum should get them, but I knew where he was coming from and I wanted them to go to Tower 20. That was a problem for management to figure out, and one of my main reasons for going to Thanksgiving that year was that I would be eating dinner with the people who ran the company and maybe I would get a chance to give them my opinion. I also wanted Crank and all the pricks at Grisdale to know who I was on Monday when we got back to work, without me telling them.

"You really do have a mother?" Bob asked me on Thursday morning as we got ready to go to Seattle.

"I didn't crawl out from under a rock." I had been telling him for years that my mother was the only family I had. "There's more to the story but that can wait until we get on the road."

"That's got me curious."

Bob dressed in his finest cowboy garb which included cowboy boots, a worked leather belt with a silver rodeo buckle, a western shirt, his good cowboy hat and silver and turquoise rings on each hand. After seeing all the women he attracted when dressed like that, I had long since quit making fun of him. Me on the other hand, I just put on what I usually wore to town, my Romeo slippers, Levis, best flannel shirt and Filson mackinaw, which was in good shape because I never worked in it. Snow had convinced me to buy a nice fedora, which I put on, but I knew I'd be the most underdressed person at the party by far. Many of the men would be wearing suits.

I drove and Bob fired up a joint when we turned onto the camp road. "So what's the mystery," he asked after we each took a hit and I passed it back to him.

"My Dad was a logger up here and was killed topping a tree before he and my mom could get married. She belongs to the family that owns the company."

"No shit! That means you belong to the family that owns the company."

"But I'm a bastard."

"Who cares? That also means that we are going to eat turkey with the people we work for."

"Yep. And have plenty of good whiskey to drink, too. Still want to go?"

"I can hardly wait to get there."

I told him more of the story as I drove. "I thought I was good keeping things to myself," was his only comment, but I figured it gave him something to think about as he watched the scenery go by.

The country roads were empty but the freeway was crowded. Driving through the sprawling suburbs was depressing. Even back then it was obvious the region was becoming a soggy version of Los Angeles. Seattle itself was a welcome sight. By the time we dropped into the Duwamish Valley and could see north several miles to downtown, the weather had improved and gaps in the clouds allowed shafts of sunlight to shine on the buildings. I'm just making this up, but because I didn't go to Seattle very often, it always seemed like something new had been built. In downtown, I took the James Street exit and started winding over Capitol Hill towards Lake Washington. Taking Madison or going through the Arboretum would have been faster but I wanted to go through the poor part of the city and show Bob where I had gone to high school. It wasn't that far out of the way. The rain scrubbed streets and neighborhoods hadn't changed. This would always be home.

As we got closer to the lake, the houses became

nicer and by the time we could see the water, they were all mansions. The one we were headed for was on the shoreline and surrounded by so many trees and shrubs you could barely see it from the street. I thought about parking out there but at the last moment turned into the driveway. My pickup looked as if it had just driven out of a mud hole, which it had, but I had as much right to park on the property as anyone else. From the number of vehicles, it looked as if half the family had arrived. We got out and as we were walking past the lush shrubbery to the entrance of the stone Tudor masterpiece built by Scottish Masons, three quick shotgun blasts greeted us from the other side of the building. "All right," Bob exclaimed.

We walked in the front door without knocking. We could hear some people down the hall in the great room, but I suspected most of the men folk were out by the lake taking turns shooting. Although I hadn't been to my grand uncle's house for Thanksgiving in a decade, I knew my mom and most of the women were in the kitchen.

Bob followed me through the dining room past two long tables already set for the feast, through double swinging doors that were propped open, and into the huge kitchen. To the side was a large breakfast nook where a dozen well dressed women of various ages sat around another large table smoking cigarettes and drinking wine or cocktails. My grandmother who I had heard wasn't in good health was sitting next to my mother, which was good, but my cousin Robert from Hollywood was there too finishing a story that had all the women laughing. Oh shit, I said to myself. I had forgotten about him.

Luckily my mother saw me first. "Eduardo!" she nearly shouted and stood to hug me. Nina had influenced both of us.

"Hello Mama," I said as I opened my arms. "Why are you crying?"

"It's so good to see you."

"You just saw me a few months ago."

"Every mother should be so lucky. That was six months ago."

Some of my aunts and cousins actually said "Ohhh, how nice." Several said hello to me.

My grandmother smiled and sat up straight. She was always good to me, and I walked around the table and pecked her on the cheek.

"I thought you were just teasing us when you said you might show up," she said. "And you brought a guest."

"Grandmother, this my friend Bob from camp."

Mama stepped in and introduced him to everyone else, sparing me the job.

"I thought you worked in our logging camp," my Aunt Liz exclaimed. "I didn't know we were in the ranching business. Of course Harold would never tell me that knowing how much I enjoy riding."

That got a little bit of a laugh and if it didn't make Bob nervous it should have.

"And this is Ed's cousin Robert," Mama finished.

"We know each other, mam," Bob said.

"What a pleasant surprise," Robert gushed.

"That it is," Bob said.

"Ladies," Robert said. "Don't be surprised if the handsome cowboy gives me a black eye. I certainly deserve one."

"You are right about that," Bob said in a way that didn't let anyone know whether he was serious or joking. "I suppose I could say we have a bone to pick but I'm not going that far."

"Oh damn," my cousin said, and everyone laughed, Bob the loudest.

The food being cooked smelled good, but familiar, and

Bob and I turned around to look into the kitchen at the same time. We couldn't believe it. There was Dodge, standing next to an oven, looking at us. He smiled, waved, shook his head and turned back to his job. His wife Alice was there too. She helped him sometimes in the cookhouse. I wondered how much my uncle paid to get them there on Thanksgiving. It was rumored that Dodge made more money than the siderods because of the overtime he put in. When I had the chance later on, I told him not to worry about keeping any secrets. That would relieve any guilt he might feel when he got back to camp and told Bee and Marge who he had seen in Seattle. I wouldn't have to tell Crank anything.

My mother looked good and I could tell she hadn't had much to drink. She didn't have an alcohol problem but she tended to drink a lot when she was on pills. She had been clean for a couple of years but I always worried that she would have a relapse. It also helped that she had been practicing psychotherapy and other forms of counseling for 20 years and was hitting her stride professionally. I hugged her again and told her I wanted to sit down and talk to her later but was going to take Bob out to the lake and introduce him to the men.

"Okay. Go out and say hello to your grandfather. He was happy to hear you might be coming this year."

I bet, I almost said. It was a fairly long walk out through the big house and down the lawn to the water. On the way out, we stopped at the bar and poured ourselves a couple of tall whiskeys. I let Bob pick out the brand. He knew them all. We passed a few smaller groups of people, younger shirttail relatives for the most part and children. Some of them I recognized and some of them I didn't. They came from California, Hawaii, Sun Valley, and New York and now were interspersed through the mansion and grounds looking at photographs and artwork on the walls, drinking and catching up. Outside, the grass was wet and spongy but a few of the younger guys were tossing a football around. There'd be a football game in a while. Had to keep up with the Kennedys. The men were down near the boathouse and dock. Three of them were holding shotguns. Four were standing around with drinks in their hands watching. Every few moments a clay pigeon or two would fly into the air and one of the guys would raise a gun and spray birdshot over the water.

My grandfather was holding a drink. All the men were dressed up but he was the most dapper one there. He got a haircut every week even though he hardly had any. I was bald thanks to him. His thin mustache was always trimmed and he looked as if he just stepped out of a movie from the thirties or forties. He wasn't related to any of the men by blood but me. He didn't work for their timber company, either. He had his own business and money. At that time he hadn't yet referred to me as "my grandson," even though I carried his family name. That would come a few years later in a letter to a friend of his I ran into on the Amazon. His back was to me as we rounded the end of the boathouse. Uncle Jack saw me first. Uncle Jack was a great uncle and although he no longer ran the company, he was still head of the family and lived in this estate. He was also ten years older than my grandfather.

"Well god damn, it's the logger of the family and a cowboy. I'm so glad you could make it." He tucked his shotgun under his left arm, barrel to the ground, and stuck out his hand. "Who's your friend?"

"Bob Smith. He's a logger too. We live in the same bunkhouse and have been friends ever since we started working up there."

I turned and greeted my grandfather. He smiled and offered his hand, too. "It's nice to see you, Edward. Say, I like that hat. It's a Stetson, isn't it?" That may have been the nicest thing he ever said to me. "I'd be happy to send you to my tailor if you want a nice jacket and trousers to go with it."

In the past I would have thought he was criticizing me about how I was dressed, and I suppose he was, but I didn't take it that way this time. I let it slide. His eyes looked tired. There was sadness in them. "No thanks, grandfather. Not this time. Maybe someday when I no longer work in the woods though."

"That would be nice," he said and we both laughed.

After the introductions were over, Uncle Jack explained how he had just gotten a new shotgun and asked if either of us would like giving it a try. I can't remember what kind of gun it was but Bob jumped at the chance.

"Do you shoot?"

"Yes, sir. I grew up in Iowa and have been hunting pheasants since I was big enough to hold a .410 to my shoulder."

That got Uncle Jack going. He hadn't been pheasant hunting in the Midwest for years, and he started asking Bob questions about specific regions and fields, some that Bob claimed he knew about and had hunted. "Let's see you shoot," Uncle Jack finally said. "How many clay pigeons do you want to try?"

"Three."

After he said pull and the machine flung them into the air, Bob waited a moment as they spread out then pulled the trigger and pumped the handle on the gun. Boom, Boom, Boom. He powdered the two front pigeons and fragmented the third. "Nice shooting," Jack congratulated him.

"That's a beautiful gun, sir. Fantastic balance. No pull. The action is super smooth. Thank you for letting me try it."

"I'm glad you liked it. Ed, how about you?"

"Sure," I said.

I didn't do as well as Bob. I missed the first one, fragmented the second, and powdered the third, which wasn't too bad.

"When did you learn to shoot?"

"Up at camp. Bob forced me to buy an old 20 gage to shoot grouse with once in a while. It's been a good year. I've shot at least six this fall."

"Does Dodge cook them for you?"

"No. Bob grills them on our barbecue. He's a good cook too."

"That sounds like fun," Uncle Jack, said. "Perhaps I'll come up and go out with you some time."

I almost suggested he take Crank along to fetch the dead birds.

A light rain started to fall and we all walked back to the house. After wiping down the guns and leaving them on a table in the den, we gathered around the bar for refills.

"Are you the Bob Smith who is tending hook on Tower 20?" my Uncle Pete asked. (He wasn't really my uncle, but a cousin.)

"Yes I am," Bob said.

"You are doing a hell of a job."

"Thank you. I've got a great crew."

"Yes, but to be getting as many loads that you do every day is fantastic."

"You are making that Washington pay. We were wondering if it was worth the investment, especially after the experiment on that big show fizzled. I thought that was crazy, but Crank talked Big Boy into it and we decided to go along with them. Those two don't make many mistakes." I knew which show they were talking about. It was so large and difficult to access that engineers wanted to contract it out to a helicopter outfit but Crank had insisted logging it with cables. "Didn't you work on that show, Ed?"

"I pulled rigging on it for a little while. It was a bitch."

"Every other rigging slinger they put on it quit," Bob

told them. "Thank God they didn't put me there."

"That's right," my uncle said. "You helped us get through that fiasco."

That was embarrassing. "I didn't know you guys kept track of individual crews and shows."

"Not all of them."

"Say, who do you think is going to get the most volume this year? Tower 20 and your friend here, or Tower 7 and Spike Larue?"

"You guys are keyed into that?"

"We sure are. I met with Crank last week in Shelton and he said he has put one hundred dollars on Tower 7. Hunt has a hundred on 20."

"That explains a lot. He seems to be helping Larue and screwing over Bob whenever he gets the chance."

"I wouldn't say that," Bob said.

"Well don't worry," Pete said. "Crank is between a rock and a hard spot. We gave him a huge quota this year."

"And a big budget by the way."

"That's right, and we know Crank wants to earn his bonus more than anything else. Apparently, some of his cows got brucellosis this year and he had to put down most of his herd. So he's not going to impede Tower 20 from getting as much wood as possible."

"We've heard all about his poor cows. He won't stop talking about them." I wanted to tell them about Red Bodene, too, but Bob would have shit.

"I hear you have your own crew now, too," my grandfather spoke up.

"Yeah. The Triple Drum. It's the smallest machine in camp."

"That's okay," Uncle Pete consoled me. "We thought that machine was headed for the scrap heap and appreciate that you are getting some production out of it."

136

"Thanks. Maybe you can get Crank to give me some new haywire. The stuff I have is rotten. I break it every time I change roads. That right there is probably worth a quarter load a day."

"Okay. I'll see what I can do but I'm sure it's the last machine in camp that Crank wants to put money into."

"You don't have to tell me that."

"Big Boy did tell us that Crank told him to credit the logs you yarded for Bob to the Triple Drum instead of Tower 20."

"I don't care who they go to. I'm not in the running for any awards. But I think 20 should get them. They had to yard them, too."

"Isn't each logging show an accounting unit?" my grandfather piped up. "Wouldn't separating out those logs create a new logging show in the books and confuse the Forest Service?"

"You have a good point, George," Pete agreed. "We want to keep things as simple as possible for our partners in the federal government. So be it. They go to Tower 20."

He was looking at Bob and me when he said that. We looked at each other and smiled.

"Thank you," Bob said. "I think I'll bet Crank a hundred dollars now."

After another stiff drink, the scene started to get psychedelic. My perception of how I fit into this family blurred. Here I was talking the nuts and bolts of the business with my relatives who ran it from their office in Seattle, and they were listening to me. Was I really an outcast? My best friend had charmed every woman and man there. The lines between them and me were shifting. Did someone put a drug into my drink, I wondered and let myself drift into the background. I wanted to talk to my mother about my father. That was the other big reason I was here.

More relatives showed up. Finally my cousin Kip and his fiancé arrived, delegating Bob's and my status as celebrities back to a sideshow where they belonged. Kip was Uncle Pete's son. He was about Robert's age and was the rising star of the family. Ivy League, MBA, smart, handsome, charismatic and now engaged to a beautiful woman equally bred and educated, their wedding announcement had taken up a full column in the *New York Times*. Just seeing them made me feel every ounce the dufus logger. I didn't know it yet but by becoming a hooktender I had cemented a place into the family lore.

At dinner I sat next to my mother. Robert had arranged for Bob to sit on the other side of the table between one of my saucier, single, older cousins and a younger, pretty one whose boyfriend was screwing around with his buddies for the weekend. We weren't at my Uncle Jack's table but that was okay. There were two big turkeys on both of them along with a leg of lamb and a huge broiled salmon plus all the fixings that made a traditional Thanksgiving meal. A couple of servers refilled glasses and brought out items as they disappeared, but Dodge stayed in the kitchen until he was called and applauded with a toast. He wasn't responsible for some of the gourmet dishes but he had been cooking turkeys here for several years I guess due to his expertise at roasting large quantities of meat.

Before we dug in, Uncle Jack made a long speech and a reverend from the biggest Episcopalian church in the city provided a longer prayer. Then there were a few toasts, to Kip, his bride to be, and to Uncle Jack of course. I was glad to be forgotten at that point. As we began eating, the noise level rose until my mom and I discovered that if we turned sideways and spoke directly to one another we were in our own sound bubble.

"Mama, I want to talk to you about my father. Can we do it now or would you prefer to do it later?"

"Now. I don't think anyone will pay attention to us."

"I broke into a filing cabinet in the office at Grisdale and stole the accident report about his death." Which wasn't quite truthful but got the point across.

"That was bold."

"I had help."

"Your friend Bob?"

"No, his girlfriend for a while, though. The secretary."

"What were you doing alone in the office with her at a time when you could rifle through company records?"

"That's a long story."

"You like her, don't you? I hear she is pretty."

"How do you know?"

"She has a reputation. Just about everyone of your uncles who work for the company has found an excuse to drop in at Grisdale at least once this last year to see her. Their wives tell me some have specifically requested she attend meetings in Shelton to take notes. She has provoked a lot of gossip these past months. She's married. They're married. Everyone thinks it's harmless."

"Okay, Okay, I've heard enough. You are blowing me away. How do you know I like her?"

"Because your best friend fell in love with her for a while and abandoned you for her. I don't know, Ed. I'm just guessing. I'm a therapist. I've been listening to convoluted love stories for a while and have heard every one there is dozens of times. Human beings are so similar to one another it's scary. You are innocent when it comes to love and women. You are so vulnerable. I worry about you. I am glad it was Bob who had an affair with her and not you."

I didn't say anything. She just looked at me.

"Honey, having sex with someone just once usually doesn't constitute a love affair."

"How do you know I had sex with her?"

139

"I'm a woman. I'm highly intuitive. And besides, why shouldn't she want you? She's a hungry woman. Probably a sex addict if not a nymphomaniac."

"Or just highly disturbed."

"I'm sure she is. I'm sure she is a lovely person, too. I'm sure I'd like to talk to her but it would take years to help her heal from whatever it is she is reacting to. In the meantime, she's a wrecking ball, to herself and to anyone who attaches to her."

"I can't believe I am having this conversation with my mother."

"Neither can I. I'm ecstatic."

"So what about my father? You have always said you loved him. Did what you have constitute an affair?"

"Yes. We were able to spend several weekends together. On Labor Day, with the help of some of my friends, I met him at a little motel on the ocean near Pacific Beach. I'll always remember that weekend. You were born nine months later. I've never had any regrets. He returned to camp a day late, and was almost fired. We spent two other weekends together after that. He drove all the way up to Seattle to be with me. We were in love, Ed. We wrote several letters to one another. I was devastated when he was killed. Afterwards, his parents were sweet enough to give me the letters I wrote to him, and I have the entire set tucked away. You can read them after I die."

"I can wait. Did he ever say anything about Crank?"

"He didn't like Crank. Crank was trying to fire him. Especially after he missed that day of work. Why do you ask?"

"The accident report was pretty explicit. Crank and a man named Sprint Jackson were with him when he died. He died doing a job Crank or Sprint should have been doing. To me it seems like Crank was negligent. I don't know. Maybe I'm just trying to find some dirt because I don't like him. I did for a while but not any more. Did he like you? Do you think he might have been hard on my dad because you two were in love?"

That got a rise out of her eyebrows. "Yes. I've always had good reason to think that. The cocky little sonofabitch made a not so subtle pass at me at the dance at the grange where I met your father. My cousins, Crank, Sprint, a few other of the boys from Grisdale, your father and I were outside passing a bottle around. Some of the folks went inside to dance. Your father disappeared to relieve himself and I found myself alone with Crank for a few minutes. He immediately put one arm around me, grabbed one of my breasts, and told me if I wanted a real man I needed to go with him to his car. I couldn't help but laugh at him; he was so ridiculous. I pushed him away. Your father came back from the outhouse a few seconds later and I pulled him inside to the dance."

"Ruby, the secretary, told me he groped her, too."

"That doesn't surprise me. Once a groper, always a groper."

We had a good laugh over that one.

"What about Sprint?"

"I didn't get to know Sprint. He was a little older and wise enough not to flirt with the daughters of the people he worked for. Your father liked him though. They were friends and he was a mentor to your dad. They had both gone to Elma High School although were four or five years apart. Both of them had been sprinters and runners on the track team. Both of them had gone to State. In fact your father may have broken some of Sprint's records at the time. But that apparently didn't bother Sprint."

"Wow, I didn't know that. That's where I got my speed."

"Men. You are all the same. I just tell you things about my love affair with your father that you never knew and what do you get excited about? That he passed down to you the talent for running fast."

That made me mad for some reason. "Why shouldn't I be glad about that?"

"I'm sorry, Ed. I was only kidding. I know it was difficult for you not knowing your father."

"It still is."

She started crying. I should have put my arm around her and told her how much I appreciated everything she had done for me but I wasn't there yet. She smiled at me through her teary eyes and told me she had to fix her makeup, then got up and left. My relatives sitting around us acted as if they barely noticed. They all knew I had an anger problem.

I turned around and ate some food. The turkey and dressing, the mashed potatoes and gravy, the green beans and dinner rolls tasted like the turkey dinner Dodge had served us at the cookhouse on Tuesday night, but I guess that was the point. Us loggers ate his grub so often we didn't know how special it was and seeing it served on silver platters didn't change that lack of respect. The salmon and lamb tasted like it came out of the cookhouse, too. I knew what the pie was going to be like.

Bob, my aunt, cousin and Robert were still carrying on. They got up and went to the living room. When I finished eating and Mama hadn't returned, I went out and joined them. They were standing with a larger group of people.

"Hey, Ed. Can I tell them the story about the crabs?" Bob asked.

"Sure. Go ahead and get some more laughs at my expense. I don't care." I went and poured myself a fresh drink and made sure I was back in time to deliver the punchline. "I had them, I'm telling you." We had told this story a few times.

We stayed with my mom the rest of the weekend. The

next night we went and saw the new Star Wars movie at the UA150 theater. The line went clear around the block but we were loaded and so was everyone else. Saturday night we went out drinking. Robert came with us for a while. We started early in the Pike's Place Market at a tavern Robert picked out called the Pigalle. It was a dive, and rough. Robert told us he would never have been able to go in there by himself or with any of his other friends but with us he felt safe. It just so happened that we ran into an acquaintance of his. A guy named Jesse who was no fairy. He was about my size, wiry, and it was obvious that the way he lived had made him tough. He was a trip. I think seeing us in there with Robert he thought we were queers so he let us know he was bisexual. But as he figured out our relationship to one another, and that we were loggers from over on the Olympic Peninsula, he rolled with it. Besides, we were buying the beer. He invited us to a party at an artist's studio in Bell Town. That scene was more to Robert's liking. He knew a lot of people there. Everyone was getting loaded on pot and coke and some people were shooting up. Jesse read his poetry. He had a lot of anger in him, which was something else we had in common. Things started getting a little weird so Bob and I left. Robert stayed there. I saw him only two more times after that. Seven years later he died of AIDS.

Bob and I walked down First Avenue to Pioneer Square and ended up at the J&M at a table with some coeds from the UW. It was a good night.

I need to take a break.

We were hung over and burned out on Sunday but Mama acquired three tickets to the Seahawks game in the Kingdome. We drank a couple of King Beers and were too tired to drive to camp when it was over so we went back to her place, slept a little and got up and left at two-thirty in the morning. Mama made coffee for us. We stopped at Hawks Prairie for another cup, then again at a quick stop in Montesano before heading up the camp road. That was at about four-thirty. We bought a case of beer, a roll of Copenhagen, and I filled up with gas. Thank God we did that. They had a security camera there, which was a fairly new innovation in the late seventies, and the cops were able to use it to confirm our story. We rolled into camp around five-thirty. It was raining hard. We carried our stuff to our hootch, set it down, and flopped on our respective bunks. Russ hadn't shown up yet, but luckily for him, he stopped in Shelton at an all night gas station with a security camera and bought the same stuff we did. Snow had spent Thanksgiving at Pierre's house and rode back to camp on the town bus that morning so he had an alibi. I fell asleep.

My nap ended an hour later when Russ crashed through the door and shouted at me to get up. Ruby had been murdered, he yelled. Ruby had been murdered! What??? I sprung off the bed, still fully dressed with shoes on, and sprinted towards the lights and noise at the Sugar Shack. Turneau was standing at the door with his arms spread out wide keeping people out. It's a crime scene he was saying. Stay out. But the door was open. I elbowed my way through the men peering around him. They were like flies. He didn't say anything specifically to me but kept saying over and over again, "It's a crime scene, stay out." I pushed him aside, stepped through the door, and stopped. Her bled out body was laying on the floor in front of me. All she had on was a bathrobe. It was open and she was naked underneath, on her back, with her arms spread wide and her legs slightly curled up under her, eerily like Jesus Christ. Her skin was white but there were dark spots on her face that may have been bruises. My eyes focused on the two-inch long gash under the edge of her ribs, left of center. It seemed like the only spot on her that was still alive. Spike Larue's knife lay in the blood beside her. The room was cold. The chill of death popped into my mind and has remained there ever since. Her eyes were open looking at the ceiling and her lips were parted, frowning.

"Why don't you close the door," I told Turneau.

"It's a crime scene," he said.

"Get someone to fetch sheets out of the bed maker's shack and hang them up so people can't stand here and stare."

"Good idea. Will you help me?"

I pushed him through the door and closed it.

I walked to the cookhouse. It was already crowded. Bob was sitting at a table by himself and I sat down next to him. He told me that he had lain on his bunk for fifteen minutes or so then got up, put his rigging on, and went over to the cookhouse a few minutes before 6 am. Dodge had looked up from the grill and smiled at him when he walked in. Bee was throwing candy bars and other goodies into the lunch sacks. Marg was setting dishes of fruit out for breakfast. He set his hat and nosebag on the table beside the door then went down to the far end of the room to the spike table to make a lunch. As he built a sandwich, Bee rang the chow bell. A few men had come in behind him. When he was done putting his lunch together, he went over to the sink next to the coffee vat and began rinsing out his steel thermos. That was when Plunger, the camp caretaker, ran into the cookhouse.

"She's dead!" he yelled. "Ruby's dead! She's been murdered!" I wonder how many times those words were shouted that morning.

"What?" Bob asked.

"She's been stabbed. She's on the floor. I was picking up the keys. The door was ajar. Sometimes she invites me in for coffee and we chat as she gets ready for work. She's there now on the floor, dead!"

145

Bob sprinted out the door and over to her place. Some men were already there and more were on the way. Men gave way and moved back for him. He knelt down outside the puddle of blood and looked at her a moment. "That's Larue's knife," he said absently. The words Spike Larue rippled through the small throng. He reached across and touched the side of her face with the back of his hand.

"Is she still warm?"

"No."

"That's too bad," a wiseass chuckled.

Bob grabbed the front of the man's jacket with two hands, lifted him off the ground, looked him in the face, and then dropped him. "EVERYBODY OUT OF HERE!" he roared. Turneau was there by then trying to get them outside but when they heard Bob they did what he said. Most of the men followed him back into the cookhouse. The crowd was gathering fast. Because Turneau wouldn't close the door, everybody was getting a look at her body and the shock was having an ugly effect. Spike Larue, Spike Larue was rippling through the noise.

"Do they think I'm going to go down and get him?" Bob asked me quietly. "I don't think he did it. He wouldn't be dumb enough to leave his knife behind. That was a set up."

"Not unless he went totally nuts."

Ruby was now the sweetest virgin that had ever hit camp. Twenty or thirty men were in there by then. More were coming up from the bunkhouses and the village. The town buses would start arriving pretty soon. Just about the time the mob was about to go off on its own and get Larue, he walked in the door.

"There he is. Grab him," someone yelled.

At least six men jumped on him. Later on, nearly everyone would admit the surprised look on his face was that of an innocent man, but nobody was operating on logic.

146

Spike fought back.

"What's going on?" he yelled when restrained.

"You murdered Ruby."

"You knifed her in the gut."

"The hell I did!"

"The hell you didn't. Your knife is laying over there beside her body."

"I lost my shank a week ago!"

"Yeah right. Somebody get some rope so we can tie him up."

"Let's string him up," a chorus of men laughed. Spike didn't have many friends. It took three men to hold him. They punched him several times. The crowd swayed back and forth as he struggled. I just sat there with Bob, watching. The homeguards from the village had taken charge. Skoot, Green Bud, and the rest of the boys were starting to roll in. "What's happening?" each man asked when he walked in. It felt like there were a hundred men in the cookhouse by then.

Someone had called the Sheriff, but it would take an hour for him to arrive. Where was Crank? I didn't think they were going to lynch Spike even though it wasn't difficult picturing him killing her, and it was hard to believe that she was dead even though I had just seen her body. She only had a few more days to work then she would have disappeared like everyone else when they quit for the season. That wasn't going to happen so nicely now.

Spike was breathing hard and his nostrils opened and closed as he strained to get free. His eyes were angry. Another town bus arrived and a fresh wave of men surged in. Then Clark came in, Spike's yarder engineer and sidekick, carrying a black powder Colt Forty-Five.

"Let him go," he demanded, pointing his gun at one of the men holding Spike. "I said let him go!"

"What gives you the right?"

"In case you're blind, this gun gives me the right."

"Maybe you helped kill her!"

"Maybe I did and maybe I'm gonna blow you away if you don't let him go." To stress his point, he fired a shot into the ceiling above them. The explosion stunned the crowd as the round tore through the ceiling and roof and showered splinters and dust on the knot of men holding Larue. Blue gunpowder smoke wafted through the room. Clark didn't know how close he was to getting his own head blown off because a faller was fetching his deer rifle from his pickup, but the men holding Spike let go. He jumped away. As Clark held the crowd back with the gun. Spike shook off their touch, stretched and rubbed himself.

"I'm getting the hell out of here," he said and crashed through the door just as the man with the rifle was sneaking onto the porch. Spike pushed the door into him, knocked him over, then jumped down the steps and landed balls out for the woods. When the faller recovered and stood up, he aimed at Spike and pulled the trigger. He later claimed it was a reflexive reaction. Spike did a forward somersault on the run and a red blotch was seen on the back of his right shoulder when he stood and resumed running. Skoot grabbed the rifle out of the faller's hands before he could shoot again. Spike was gone.

Men were yelling to go after him, but Clark had backed onto the porch and told everyone to stay where they were. There was no question that he meant business.

"We can't let him get away."

"Yes we can."

That was when Crank finally showed up. He walked between Clark and the mob and yelled at everyone to shut up. "That's right. Nobody is going after him, and put those guns down."

Men were yelling at him.

"I know a lot of you don't like him, but we're loggers not law enforcement officers, and they are on the way. It's their job to find him, not ours."

"You don't have any authority in this."

"The hell I don't. Any of you miss one minute of work chasing him you better stop at the office to pick up your last check when you get back."

There was a lot of bitching but when they realized that the snow could start falling any time and that they wouldn't be able to collect unemployment during winter shutdown if they were fired, they felt Crank's hand gripping their nuts.

"Good. Now put that gun away, Clark, and everybody get ready for work. We'll start an hour later than normal but you'll be paid for eight." What a concession.

Quiet Bob went outside and stood in the rain. It was coming down hard. He was standing alone off to the side away from other men as they left the cookhouse. Light was ebbing back into the sky revealing puddles and slanting streaks of water. The buildings looked dead and had taken on the appearance of a temporary movie set. I filled his thermos with coffee, grabbed his nosebag and boots, and carried them out to him.

"Here you go, comarada," I said as I handed him his rigging. "The Canyou River crummy is probably waiting for you."

"I want to kill the fucker who did it," he said as he walked away.

"Me too."

That was the worst day I ever had in the woods. When the crummy stopped at the landing, blasts of wind howling across the denuded slopes kept rocking it back and forth and none of us got out. I sat up front on the passenger side with my fists doubled up, slowly pounding my thighs.

Buffy threw on the air brakes and slumped over the

steering wheel. "Do I really got to work in this mess today, boss?" he asked, looking at the Triple Drum. The bastard contraption had rolled off the lowboy once and the cab, the size of a large coffin, was tilted inward at an odd angle. The glass had been busted out of the windows too, so there would be no escaping the wind and rain. I knew Buffy wished he were still a chaser. Then he could stand next to the landing fire and look at the trees, mellow out in between turns, and not have to worry about the men whose lives were in his hands, not to mention his own. The previous week the butt of a wild log punched in the metal screen welded over the front window. "When a man is killed in the woods all his friends can take the rest of the day off so why can't we do that for the secretary?"

"Crank doesn't give a fuck. All he wants is his bonus," I told him.

Buffy looked at his watch.

"What time is it?" I couldn't stop thinking about Ruby. She wouldn't be in the office to warm me up after work.

"Ten to Nine."

I let another half hour slip by.

"No use fucking the dog. Might as well get it over with."

Buffy opened the door and slid out, taking his raingear with him.

"LET'S GO YOU ASSHOLES," I yelled as I pounded on the window between the men in back and me.

"Fuck you!" one of them replied. "We need a few more minutes."

"I was only seeing if you guys were still awake," I growled more compassionately. I looked at the cold decks. We didn't have a loader. Instead, we had a skidder with a set of hydraulic grapples at the end of a hydraulic arm that made it look like a scorpion. The man operating the machine grabbed the logs after they were un-belled, pulled them down the road a ways and stacked them in the ditch. They were Crank's ace in the hole. If he needed more wood to reach his quota after the snow began to fall, he'd plow the road so that a loader and a contingent of trucks could get in and haul the wood out before Christmas. If he didn't need the logs, he'd let them sit all winter then load them out in the spring when they would be a nice start on next year's count. Watching them grow the past few weeks had been gratifying but did little for me that morning. Looking back on it, I still get embarrassed knowing how I was helping Crank.

"Do you really think he killed her?" Buffy asked after crawling into his raingear.

"I don't know," I answered.

"I can't figure it out." With that, he slammed the door and trudged through the mud to the yarder.

"Neither can I," I mumbled then jumped out of the crummy myself. Before putting on my raingear, I turned in a slow circle, surveying the show as I did every morning while windmilling my right arm in big loops and massaging my shoulder with my left hand.

As Buffy topped off a tank of hydraulic fluid, I wondered if a stream of cold water was trickling down his neck and if needles of cold air were poking through the holes in his raingear like they were mine. Before he got in the cab, he sprayed ether into the engine's air filter, and when he pressed the ignition button we all were hoping the Triple Drum wouldn't start. It never did the first try. He let off a moment then tried again. And again. On the third try, black smoke wheezed from the exhaust stack and with the sound of a cement mixer full of dry gravel, the machine cleared its throat and started to rumble. The exhaust turned lighter and chugged out faster and faster until it was a steady stream. Buffy looked out the window and frowned. Now he had to run the bitch all day.

I rummaged through the toolbox in the back of the crummy until I found a new chainsaw file. Usually, I sat in the crew compartment, drank a cup of coffee, and bullshit the rigging crew a few minutes, but not this day. I stuck my head in the door and told them that they better be headed for the brush before I got to the tailend. I then went over to the yarder and lifted a coil of haywire onto my shoulder. Without the usual last minute lecture to Buffy, I walked up the road.

"I can ship that back on the rigging for you," Buffy yelled after me when he realized that I was going to carry the coil to the tailend. I didn't reply, thinking that perhaps pain would drive the picture of her corpse from my head.

A couple hundred yards up the road, I turned off and climbed through the stumps and rocks to the spine of the ridge. I couldn't hear my crew above the yarder's engine and I wondered if they had gotten out of the crummy. But when I was near the top of the hill, I heard Percy, the rigging slinger, blow the whistles for Buffy to run the rigging back to where he and the chokerman were waiting. We were hi-leading, and the yarder ran louder as the engineer wound on the long cable that pulled the chokers back to them. Another whistle blew signaling Buffy to stop and there was silence as the two men wrapped their snares around logs. My mind pushed against the load on my back, but it didn't do much good at easing the other load. I had mastered logging's physical aspects long ago. Who murdered her?

When I arrived at the first tailhold stump, I threw the coil off my shoulder and caught my breath. Rainwater had already worked through my boots and socks. Bracing against a gust of wind, looking into the grey soup, I felt as if I was standing on the edge of the world. The drops of water pattered into my rubber clothing and hardhat like tiny drumsticks. It dripped off the brim of my hardhat in the same spot so steadily that to keep from being hypnotized I had to force myself not to watch. The wind pushed the water up and under my brain bucket then gravity pulled it down through the stubble of hair on the sides of my head, over my neck and under my coat where it mingled with the sweat in my clothes. It formed icy rivers on the skin of my face and dripped off my chin. I pulled off my gloves, fished under my rain jacket for my snoose, and shoveled a load behind my lower lip. Before I could stick the lid back on the can, a gust of wind blew it out of my hands. The shiny round lid sailed out and drifted downward into the lee of the ridge. I watched it disappear. Normally, something like that provoked a rigging fit, but that day I just shrugged my shoulders, set the little can on a stump, and covered it with a flat rock.

Whistles blew. The haulback that ran 1,500 feet from the tower to the tailend where I was standing, through two blocks then back to the chokers, tightened as the mainline pulled the turn to the landing. Buffy kept tension in the long cable to brake the wood as it traveled down hill. Still, the cable picked up speed until the wheels in the blocks were a blur. There was a loud snap and a pecker pole they choked broke in two leaving a four-foot chunk in the snare. The log in the other choker, a bunk log, started to slide out of the choker. Stay on, I told it. The log stopped sliding and the choker retightened further up the log. The rigging didn't even slow down when it pulled into the log again and flung it end for end into the air and down the hill. The bouncing cable slapped the blocks up and down on the roots of the stumps. The straps holding the blocks to the stumps dug deeper into their notches. The log flew to the end of the choker and was yanked to a stop like a dog on a leash. It fell to the ground sideways and started rolling itself up inside the choker. When there was no more slack, the rigging lunged into it again and this time threw the log into space as if it were a yo-yo. The lines quivered and sang like a giant harp. The vibration traveled through the nearest tailhold stump into the ground and up my legs. I never tired of watching a big log go in. The chunk in the other choker flew around it like a sparrow harassing a raven. When the rigging got to the landing, Buffy slowed it down and pulled the log gently into the shoot. Too bad he's so spacey, I thought. Why did somebody kill her?

Snow was no longer the chaser. The regular meals, steady work, and sleep helped him straighten up, and when he was back in shape, Crank put him pulling rigging on another crew. Our new chaser walked out onto the landing and unbelled the chokers at a leisurely pace. At least he was consistent and could make good coils. After he walked back into the clear, Buffy went ahead on the haulback and the cable ran through the blocks in the other direction. I watched the two men set their chokers. It wasn't a bad crew. We got the job done. But when Percy blew in three whistles for Buffy to reel in the wood, the rigging just sat there. The men on the landing appeared to be the size of large ants and I saw that Buffy was out of the yarder standing next to a fire. "GODDAMNIT GET BACK IN THE YARDER YOU SPACEY SONOFABITCH!" I yelled but the wind blew my words in the opposite direction. The slinger blew in three more shorts. Buffy heard them this time, scrambled up on the yarder, and went ahead on the turn. I watched another turn go in, and another, until a chill slapped me back to my senses. Obediently, I walked over to the old tailhold stump, dismantled the block and strap, swung the block over my shoulder, and started back past the tailholds in use to the stump that would anchor my next road. The block weighed over eighty pounds and the strand of wire that held the pin in the gooseneck was scratching me behind the ear. I didn't notice the dead root sticking out of the ground. As I fell, I rolled in order to throw the block off my back, but a jolt of pain shot through my bad shoulder when I hit the ground.

"FUCK!" I yelled, rising to my knees. She wasn't going to be there to give me a massage. I didn't care what my mother had said. I grabbed my hardhat with both hands, lifted it over my head, and pounded it onto the block, "WHY? WHY? WHY?" I screamed with each blow. That was called a rigging fit.

An hour or so before quitting time, I saw Hunt driving up the road in his pickup followed by a cop in a police car. I walked down to the road and met them. The deputy got out of his car when he saw me. Hunt rolled down his window. "It's your turn to talk to the Sheriff," he said. "They're questioning everybody who might have been in camp when she was killed."

"What about the crew? Should they keep working?"

"Sure, why not, I'll stay here and babysit them for a half hour then let them slack off."

I grabbed my nosebag out of the front of the crummy. The deputy made me open it up so he could look inside before I crawled in back of his cruiser. Before he let me get in, he asked me to take my raingear off so I didn't mess up the seats. We didn't talk during the ride back to camp. He was probably a local boy and had gone to high school with some of the guys I worked with.

Camp was a zoo. The sheriff had set up a command post in the Rec Hall. Every television station and half the radio stations from Seattle to Portland must have had crews there. I'm sure most of the newspapers had sent reporters, too. Nobody had spotted Larue. He was a celebrity now. The reporters had already interviewed dozens of people who didn't like him. They had heard how he had been harassing Ruby since he first laid eyes on her. Although not confirmed by an autopsy, everyone knew she had been killed with the knife that Spike liked to intimidate people with. Turneau was outside of the office with a bunch of media types comparing Spike to John Turnow, the legendary outlaw who the authorities had ambushed and killed near Grisdale in 1917. I didn't have to see or hear or read the stories on the nightly news to know what was going on. Spike's trial was going to be over before they caught him. He knew what was going to happen. That is why he ran.

The deputy escorted me into the building. He didn't take me into the gym where tables had been set up and people in uniforms were sitting around radios and maps. Instead, I was put in a smaller room off the entrance, a windowless storage room that was being used for "interviews." There was a small table with a tape recorder on it and a few chairs. I sat in one of them. The deputy remained standing. Almost as soon as we got there, a woman in plain clothes followed us in. Lorraine Goodwell. That was the first time I saw her.

She turned on the tape recorder and read me my rights, explaining to me that it was a routine formality in this case. I realize now that she was trying to be a lot smoother than I gave her credit for. Her hair was pulled tight behind her head. She didn't have much makeup on. Her clothes were an attempt at a sexless replica of a man's suit, as if she were in the city, but she couldn't quite project the sterile image being fed to us in those days of what a liberated woman was supposed to look like. Hearing how I could request an attorney didn't bother me. It had been said to me before, and I wanted them to find Ruby's killer.

She had done a little bit of homework and let me know that she knew I had been arrested in Bremerton for assault but that the charges had been dropped in a pre-trial hearing.

"Is there anything you want to say about that?"

"No. They told me it would be removed from my record."

"There's more than one record, Mr. Knockle. I hope that doesn't surprise or upset you."

I didn't say anything. She then focused on the crime at

hand, and I answered her questions to the best of my ability for an hour or so. She wanted to hear everything I knew about Spike and my version of how Spike had harassed Ruby. It was obvious she had already heard lots of stories, and she was particularly interested in the time when Spike got on the radio in the crummy after work and said in a deep, ominous voice, "Here we come, Ruby. We're coming to get you." Not only was that broadcast to the central radio near her desk but to every mobile radio in all the crummies full of men heading back to camp. When she walked into the cookhouse that night, Spike asked her real loud, "Well, how was it?"

"What do you mean?" she asked.

"Whatever it was they was coming to get you for."

"Spi–ike!" she whined.

I told Goodwell I didn't think anyone thought he was serious.

"I fail to see how a woman being harassed in a logging camp is humorous," she snapped.

"You don't see me laughing about it, do you?" I snarled back at her.

"Did you think Ruby was sexy?" she suddenly changed tack.

"Yeah. Why wouldn't I?"

"Did you like her?"

I didn't answer that one so quickly. "Yeah. I liked her."

She paused and looked at me. Then she started asking questions about her affair with Bob. That's when I started getting cautious. She kept firing questions at me. Her voice wasn't exactly emotionless. She couldn't hide her contempt for the men I worked with and me. I have to admit I didn't like having to answer a woman this way either. She wanted to know about what I had done the previous weekend, with whom, and the precise details and timing of our return to camp. From her questions I figured she had already talked to Bob, but I chuckled to myself because I was able to figure out he only told her he had gone to Seattle with me to have Thanksgiving dinner with my family. He hadn't told her who that family was. Dodge hadn't told her either. It was my card to play.

She switched back to asking about Bob and Ruby breaking up. It got on my nerves. "You say you liked Ruby, Ed. Were you jealous of Bob, or Ruby?"

"Where are you going with this?"

"I want to find out who killed her, Ed."

"I can tell you that Bob didn't do it, and I didn't do it either."

"Why should I believe that? You may have had time to murder her after you got back to camp. She hadn't been dead long when Mr. Waller found her. Believe me Ed, after the lab work is done we will know the time she died. Did you ever have sexual relations with her?"

That came out of left field along with the realization that I was a suspect.

"I don't have to answer that. You told me I had a right to an attorney and I want to call mine now. Am I under arrest?"

She didn't answer my question. "You have an attorney? Who is it?"

"J.T. Brown." She starred at me as if she thought I thought she was stupid, which gave me some satisfaction. Brown had made a name for himself recently for winning the acquittal of a man charged with a series of rapes.

"Why would a juvenile delinquent from Bremerton like you have an attorney like J.T. Brown?"

"You don't even know who I am, do you?" I stood up and shouted. "Not that it matters to you or me but it might to your boss."

"Sit back down, you dumbshit," the deputy barked.

I could feel veins bulging out on my face and neck, beads of sweat boiling out of my scalp, and saliva seeping into the corners of my mouth.

Goodwell had jumped out of her chair, too, and had reached under her suit jacket for her gun but hadn't pulled it out. She was shocked and surprised and that was enough for me. I sat back down, praying that Bob didn't kill Ruby.

"Whose house do you think we had Thanksgiving dinner in?" I was barely able to spit out. "To give you a clue go find the names of the people who own stock in the company that owns this building," I continued more calmly. "It's a private company and the list is short." My mom's name was on it. "And J.T. Brown got me out of that trouble in Bremerton."

"Stay here, Mr. Knockle. I'll be back in a little while."

She left the room, leaving me with the deputy. The adrenalin dissipated and left me feeling exhausted, and disappointed for losing control. I had never wanted to act like a rich brat. After a while I stood up to leave. "Where are you going?" the uniform asked. "I need to take a leak." He looked at me a moment then told me to follow him to the can. I knew better than to make a ruckus. When we got back, I sat and waited for at least another hour before Goodwell returned and told me I could leave.

"I'm still calling him," I told her as I walked out.

"Do whatever you think you need to do, Mr. Knockle."

And I did. My bunkhouse had been searched, but I found his card in my wallet (We never carried wallets in the brush.) and walked back up to the phone booth next to the Rec Hall. I crowded to the front of the line of reporters waiting to use it. There was a 10-minute limit. Mr. Brown didn't pick up until I started leaving a message on his recorder.

He told me my mother had already called and given

him a heads-up. Chalk another one up to her intuition. I told him they were suspicious of Bob and me. They would be suspicious of everyone he said, but they couldn't do anything without evidence and so far the cards were stacked against Larue. He told me that because my family was one of the biggest employers in the county, they probably wouldn't give me a hard time again unless they thought they had a reason to. In fact, he doubted if they would interview me again. He said if they did, and I wanted to, I could give him a call and he'd jump in his car and head down. In the meantime, he told me not to tell them anything I didn't want to.

I'm taking another break.

It was after seven o'clock when I got off the phone. Normally the cookhouse would have been closed by then but it was still open for the cops and media. Dodge was feeding them chicken, mashed potatoes, gravy and pies. I asked him if he had seen Bob or Snow, and he said they had come in for super at the regular time. That was it. On the way back to the bunkhouse, I swung past the parking lot and saw that Bob's and most of the other rigs were gone. Had I known where everyone went, I would have followed. Russ's rigging clothes were hanging above the heater but Bob's weren't. Neither were Snow's over at his bunkhouse. I felt left out. I didn't want reporters and camera crews following me into the latrine so I didn't take a shower. I changed into some clean rigging and resumed the position I was in that morning when Russ woke me up. As I fell asleep, I drove out the image of Ruby on the floor by imagining Spike running through the woods with a hole in his shoulder like a wounded elk, pursued by hunters who would finish the job when they caught up to him. I can't really remember what I thought about as I fell asleep that night twenty-five years ago but it does sound poetic.

I opened my eyes about ten-thirty and saw Quiet Bob and Snow standing in the hootch. They were wet, in their winter rigging, and Bob was pulling a bottle of Wild Turkey out of his locker.

"We found him," Snow told me.

"Who, Larue?"

"Yeah. He's dead."

"No shit?"

"He died while we were there, just after we gave him a drink of water."

"Where was he?"

"Over the ridge from the old Discovery Mine in a cabin in the national park that he told me about when I worked with him."

Snow filled in more details. "It was a nice shack built out of tree limbs, long cedar shakes and some plastic tarps. They even had an airtight stove. Too bad we didn't get there sooner. We could have built a fire and warmed the place up. He might have survived."

"Now, we have to tell the Sheriff," Bob continued. Do you want to have a drink with us first?"

"Sure. He's going to be mad as hell."

"They didn't ask me if I knew where he was headed," Bob said after taking a swig.

"Would you have told him?"

"Maybe."

I stood up and Snow passed the bottle to me.

Before they left, I took Mr. Brown's beat up card out of my wallet and handed it to Bob. "Take this. You may need it. That detective bitch got pushy when she questioned me. It sounded like she thinks you or I may have killed Ruby. Now they are going to think you killed Spike. I've already talked to the lawyer on the phone. He's on standby."

"Thanks."

I couldn't go back to sleep after they left. Russ returned before Bob did. I told him the news about Larue but Russ was drunk and couldn't stay awake until Bob got back. It must have been 2 am when he walked back in.

"The Sheriff threatened to charge Snow and me with tampering with evidence and obstruction of justice. When I told him I wanted to call that attorney you turned me on to, his attitude changed and he wanted to know if Brown's name and phone number were written in the latrine. At least he has a sense of humor, but then he's a politician. Lorraine Goodwell is a ball buster though. I told them I'd lead them up to Spike's body at first light so I better get a couple hours of sleep. You're welcome to come along."

"No thanks. I don't need to see another dead body."

"That thirty-thirty put a nasty hole in his shoulder. He was one tough dude to make it all the way up there."

It didn't seem like Bob was sad about Ruby at the moment, either. He and I took another pull off the bottle, then he turned the light off and went to bed.

I went to sleep thinking of Spike again. Had the bullet shattered his shoulder bone? I wondered. I knew what that felt like. A mile past the end of the lake the ground started rising. The valley narrowed and the terrain became more rugged. At some point the pain, fatigue, and cold must have gotten too intense to ignore. Did he know he was going to die? Did he know when he passed the point of no return? It was illegal to build cabins and hunt in the park, but that was probably why he and his brother did it. Perhaps they had a stash of matches, cans of food, wool blankets and other survival gear. Perhaps he thought he could get warm in the hootch, sleep and be able to heal without medical attention. But when he got there he could only collapse on the dirt floor and die. You had to hand it to him though. He had escaped the cops.

As we were milling around our crummies in the morning, stalling, the sheriff led a long caravan of vehicles out of camp. Goodwell was in the front seat with him. Bob was in back. There were forest rangers, park rangers, search and rescue, and a meat wagon to carry the body back to town. Crank was in the procession, too. Spike hadn't been killed logging, so Crank wasn't giving anyone time off. However, Clark and most of the other men on his crew didn't come to work so my guys and I worked on Tower 7 that day. I would have rather stayed on the Triple Drum. None of us worked very hard. Everyone was praying for snow. By the time we got in that night, Spike's body had been recovered and the media circus had disbanded. Only one Sheriff's car was there, Lorraine Goodwell's. She was still asking questions.

The word was that there was confusion about the correlation of the temperature inside the Sugar Shack and the temperature of her body when the cops arrived and started investigating her murder. Plunger had told Goodwell that when he opened her door, it was hot inside which was strange because usually it was cool. Goodwell learned that Ruby always slept with her window open and barely turned on her heater after she woke up. Ruby had always said she was hot blooded and attributed it to being one quarter Native American. I figured she was talking about something else. Anyway, the gas heater was still going when the cops arrived and secured the crime scene but while Turneau was standing guard with the door open, the hootch had probably cooled off into the forties. After I had closed the door, the temperature had shot up into the mid-seventies. She had the same kind of heater in her place that we had in the bunkhouses. Late at night that time of year, with a window open and the heater off, the temperature inside one of those buildings would drop into the thirties. Goodwell had come back up to camp with some scientist types to run heat experiments. It wouldn't do them any good, J.T. Brown told me later. The implication was that whoever killed Ruby was smart enough to turn her heater on full blast just to make life difficult for the cops. They'd never be able to pinpoint the time of her death without a shadow of a doubt. The other implication was that a person that crafty would never have left his knife behind, but according to the press, Spike was guilty of murder and the Sheriff was getting comfortable with that conclusion. So far, the faller who shot Larue was the only person who had been arrested, and he was already out on bail.

Earlier that day, after Bob led the recovery team to Spike's body, he returned to camp and drove his pickup over Spoon Creek Pass to his show. That let him get back to Grisdale in time to walk to the cookhouse with me. Snow sat down with us, and Bob told me to eat quick because they wanted to talk to me in private about something important. The three of us walked out together less than fifteen minutes later. We passed Russ who was headed in to eat, so we had the hootch to ourselves for a few minutes. Snow lit a joint and passed it to me.

"Guess what?" Bob said. "Larue found the treasure he was looking for and he told us where he stashed it before he died."

"You're bull shitting me."

"I shit you not, brother."

Snow cut in. "When we opened the door to his hut and shined our flashlights inside, we found him laying face down on the ground, not on one of the plank bunks on the wall. He looked dead. The back of his coat was soaked with blood. Then he groaned and tried turning onto his side to look at us. Bob helped him over then held him there. The front of his shoulder was a mess of bloody clothing, raw flesh, chunks of bone, and dirt. He wanted water. I grabbed a rusty can on a shelf and went outside to a pond near there. Bob lifted his head so he could drink. I gave him only a couple of sips. He coughed and more blood oozed out.

"'Treasure,' Spike said when he caught his breath."

"What?" I asked.

"'Treasure, dammit, open your ears,' he told us again, in the old mine, 43 paces in, three feet down. He told us it was ours, that he waited too long, and that he didn't kill Ruby. Then he asked for more water. We gave him another drink. This time he didn't stop coughing until he reached up with his good arm, grabbed the flap of Bob's coat, and died."

"And you believe him," I asked after a few moments. Don't you think he might have been pulling your leg so he could have the last laugh? Don't you think he would have told Clark?"

"He was fucking Clark's wife. Why would he tell him? We won't know if he was bullshitting us unless we go look. Are you coming with us?"

"When are you going?"

"Now."

"It's dark. The Discovery Mine is way the fuck up there!"

"It's not that bad. We walked past it last night, but when it snows we won't be able get up there until spring."

"There could be a lot of pretty coins in that hole," Snow said as he passed the joint to me again. "Gold is the most perfect substance in the world."

"You used to say that about pussy."

"You can't always count on pussy," he smiled.

"Okay. Now that you got me thinking about it, I'll go."

"Pussy or gold, eat now or later?" Bob asked as we grabbed our coats, raingear and flashlights. That became our motto for the night.

On a whim I pulled the 20 gauge out of my locker.

"I hope you aren't planning on using that on me, Ed," Snow laughed.

"Not unless you try to take my half, or third I should say."

"Thanks. Now I can't turn my back on you either," Bob said.

We laughed as we got in his truck. On the way out of the yard, we robbed a couple of shovels and a pulaski from our crummies.

As we drove north past the lake, Snow and I speculated about how much money we might find and what we would do with it. The rain had stopped, which was good, and the wind was still gusting hard. The clouds had broken apart and waves of moonlight flooded the valley. The remaining blocks of old growth looked like regiments of giants standing in the night. We passed Wynoochee Falls and the road got steeper as it wound up to a pass. Near the top we turned north onto a spur that ended near the edge of the Olympic National Park. Bob parked at a wide spot in the road. We slid out and grabbed the tools in the truck bed. Before closing the driver's door, Bob reached behind the seat for a double bitted axe.

We used our flashlights when we started climbing the half-assed trail, but there was enough moonlight so we turned them off. The miners must have been animals. The trail was steep and I sweated like a pig as usual. At a clearing we found the remains of an old log cabin. The mouth of the mine was uphill from there so we had to make another steep climb to the flat space on top of the tailings in front of the hole. It reminded me of the slit under Ruby's rib cage and the cool air coming out felt like the air in the Sugar Shack.

"How about I stand guard out here while you guys go in and get it?"

"You afraid of a little dark?" Snow laughed at me.

"That's a lot of dark in there."

We shined our flashlights down the tunnel and Bob started in, counting paces. I tried to act cool as I followed him and Snow. The cave swallowed the beams of our flashlights. "This is like the movies," I said, joggling Bob's count. "Shut up," he barked. "Did I skip a number or count one twice?" "Just start where you think you left off," Snow said. "There's little chance your paces are the same as LaRue's." So when Bob resumed we followed. By the time he reached 43 it seemed as if we had gone in a mile. "Right here!" He struck the floor of the tunnel with his shovel, but it was solid rock. We scratched around for a soft spot where someone might have dug a hole or found an existing one. Snow struck one near the side under a low pile of rubble. "Here it is." He said and began picking at the rock with the tip of his shovel. Bob joined him. I leaned the shotgun against the wall of the cave, got down on my knees and began to lift the larger stones out of the hole with my hands.

Snow's shovel stuck something that sounded hollow. After excavating several scoops of gravel, we saw the top of a two and a half gallon paint bucket, then another one next to it. After a few more moments, I was able to find the handles and lift them out. They were heavy and felt as if they were nearly full. Spike had taped the lids down with massive amounts of grey duct tape.

"Let's take them outside."

Snow and Bob each grabbed a bucket and I followed behind with my shotgun and Bob's axe. We left the shovels behind. It felt good to get outside, and we carried the buckets down to the lower clearing. Bob held his big electric light while Snow and I sliced the tape with our pocket knives and ripped the lids off. There it was, treasure in the form of thousands of antique gold and silver coins worth hundreds of thousands of modern paper dollars. Snow dipped two handfuls out of one of the buckets and let the money run slowly through his fingers. I didn't know why I was so happy, but I was. I picked one big gold piece out, held it up to the light and screamed like an idiot. Bob held some in his cupped hands and jingled them up and down. "I like the feel of that," he said, then started laughing his guts out. We all did. "That Goddamned Spike," each one of us shouted a few times.

After acting like children for several minutes, we collected the coins we had dropped on the ground and put them back into the buckets.

"How should we divide this up?" Snow wondered out loud.

"We need to do some research," Bob said. "There is a small fortune here. I think we better go to town and get a motel room tonight and sort out the coins. Hell, there are 20 dollar gold pieces in there 100 years old. Can you imagine what one of those babies is worth now? There are coins in there from all over the world, from countries that don't exist anymore. We're going to have to appraise the value of each coin. That's going to take time. To hell with work tomorrow."

"How many ways should we split it up?"

"What do you mean?"

"Spike had a kid, didn't he? Shouldn't she get some of it?"

"That's true. You're right. She should get a share. We're going to have to think about that."

"Don't worry about it, boys. I'm saving you the trouble. I'm taking it all."

We didn't have to look to see who was speaking. Each one of us had heard that cackle thousands of times, but the three of us turned around in unison and saw Crank standing ten yards away at the edge of the glow from our lantern and flashlights, pointing a .38 caliber revolver in our direction. He could have shot us while our backs were turned but he wanted to rub it in our faces how he had gotten the upper hand,

and in the next second I realized he was pointing the pistol directly at me most likely because I was standing closest to the tree the shotgun was leaning against. I wanted to look at my gun but couldn't even turn my eyeballs. He was going to shoot me first.

"Go ahead and take the money," Snow said.

"What? Just like that? You guys wouldn't mind? That's awful kind of you. Maybe you'd carry it down the hill for me."

"Sure, why not?"

"Do you think I'm that stupid, Snow?" he laughed.

"Then what are you going to do, kill us?"

"Bingo."

"You killed Ruby, didn't you," Bob growled.

"Why would I want to kill that cow?"

"Because she wouldn't let you fuck her."

"Like she did the rest of the camp?"

"You couldn't even rape her. She kicked you in the balls and got away."

"Where did you hear that from, Cowboy Bob? I've been telling everyone I think you might have killed her. I liked Spike. It would be sad to see him take the rap for something he didn't do."

"You killed my father, too," I shouted, suddenly able to move my jaw.

"You dumb bastard, Knucklehead, I didn't kill your daddy. That's right, I know who you are. You look just like him except he had hair, and I didn't have to kill him. He was so stupid he killed himself and maybe I let him. But I am going to kill you, so get ready to meet him."

At that moment, Snow raised his arms in the air, bellowed like an angry bear, and ran straight at Crank, so Crank swung his gun away from me and shot him. I still couldn't move, but, in a blur, Bob stepped towards me and pushed. I felt myself falling towards the tree. I heard Crank fire his pistol again and then again and felt hot lead whizzing by within inches of my head. I landed on the ground with my arms stretched out towards the butt of the gun. I grabbed it and as I rolled and turned towards Crank, I saw Bob out of the corner of my eye swing the axe overhead and throw it at him. As I leveled the shotgun towards Crank, he shot at Bob and the side of my best friend's head turned into a red smear. I squeezed the trigger but it didn't depress. The safety was on. In the same second that I flicked it open with my thumb, Crank pointed his pistol at me and the axe hit him in the head. The tool had cartwheeled too far for the blade to strike first but the top of the axe head struck his face. It was like getting hit in the head with a hammer. He staggered back a couple steps and caught himself before he fell. He slumped forward with his hands on his knees, the .38 still in his right hand. He shook his head once then stood up straight and raised his pistol at me again. This time when I squeezed the trigger the 20 gauge discharged its load of birdshot into his upper thigh. That leg flew back like he was in a Kung-Fu movie, kicking at something behind him, and the rest of his body spun forward with equal speed face first into the ground. The echo of my gun rumbled down the valley. In the quiet that followed, I stood up and felt wetness below my crotch. It was warm, too. Had I been shot? But when I looked down, I saw that I had pissed my pants.

Snow moaned. I walked over to him. He was lying there watching Crank who also was still alive dragging himself towards his pistol that was about three feet in front of him.

"Kill him," Snow said hoarsely.

But I didn't have to, or rather I already had. As I contemplated shooting him again, his heart pumped the rest of his blood out a severed artery in his leg. I had a few seconds when I could have put a tourniquet on it, but the thought of trying to save him didn't enter my mind.

I wish I had had the chance to save Bob but there was no question he was dead. I wish I could have said something to him, told him what it meant to be his friend and thanked him for sacrificing his life for me, but perhaps it was better this way because I have been telling him those things most of my life. I gave up trying not to cry for him and for Ruby. It all poured out until I finally heard Snow.

"Ed, Ed the Head. Get me out of here. Don't leave me in the boonies."

Crank's bullet had gone all the way through his gut without hitting his backbone or any major blood vessels. While I carried him piggyback down the mountain, he hallucinated that he was in Vietnam. I learned that the first Ed the Head had been wounded in a battle and had died while Snow was carrying him to a helicopter. Now Ed the Head was carrying him, which was confusing. He laughed and cried about it then got religious on me. It wasn't amusing for me at the time because I had to concentrate to keep from falling or dropping him. I was also stressed because I remembered we had driven up there in Bob's truck and I didn't have the keys. I didn't say anything about that to Snow. At least I hadn't locked the passenger door and was able to set him on the seat when I got him to the truck.

"Go get the treasure," he said. "I don't want this to be a complete waste."

"It already is," I told him. "But I got to go up there and get Bob's keys."

"Good. Bring the money back, too. I'll wait here."

"OK," I said.

When I arrived at the top of the hill again, Bob's electric lantern was still glowing although not as brightly, and it was easy to imagine that his spirit was hovering above his body like Jed's had. I thought I could feel him watching me. I didn't pay any attention to Crank.

"Hey Buddy," I said as I knelt beside Bob and went through his pockets. "I'm sorry I'm leaving you up here with that scumbag. Watch my back, okay? But I don't have to tell you that. I'll come back later with some of the guys and we'll carry you down in a stretcher. Thanks for saving my life." Talking like that to him made me feel better. I wish I could have told him I would always carry him inside of me and that he would always be a part of my life, but I guess I didn't know it at the time. "Adios, companero," I said after I found the keys.

When I got back to the truck again, I put the buckets on the tailgate then slid them into the bed. I opened the door to the cab and saw that Snow had slumped over sideways. I was afraid he had died, too, but he opened his eyes.

"It's about time you got back," he said.

"That's easy for you to say sitting here on your ass."

"My gut is killing me."

"Let's get the hell out of here."

I drove to Turneau's house in the village and woke him up. It wasn't midnight yet. I told him Snow needed a ride to the hospital in the ambulance. I told him not to bother to call Crank. That Crank and Bob were dead and laying on the ground at the Discovery Mine. I told him to call the sheriff's office and tell them there had been a shooting at Grisdale and that I'd wait by the office for them to arrive.

It took Turneau only 30 minutes to wake some other people up, make the call, wrap Snow in a bandage, and load him in the ambulance. After they left, I called Mr. Brown. He told me not to give the gold to the cops or I'd never see it again. We devised a plan where I put it in my truck, parked the rig on the road to the village and hid the key in an empty can of Copenhagen for him. He'd leave for Grisdale immediately and before he came to the office to find me he'd transfer the buckets to his trunk. After doing what he said, I went back to the bunkhouse, changed my pants, and then got ready for the next flurry of shit.

Lorraine Goodwell was the first to arrive. I told her what had happened but when she started asking questions like where was the gold and silver, I told her I wasn't going to talk to her anymore until my attorney got there. This time she arrested and handcuffed me. I had to sit in the back of her car for a couple of hours until Brown arrived. He took care of everything from then on.

Crank's people buried him without ceremony. Snow was in the hospital for a month; then he stayed with Pierre and Kona until he was well enough to get around. Quiet Bob's entire family came out from Iowa to retrieve his body. I knew that Bob was always writing letters, but I was surprised to find out how much information he put in them. His people knew everything about Snow, me, and the rest of the boys. They treated us all with a lot of respect so I think he must have cleaned up the details. They told us that Bob had always wanted to be a cowboy, which he was for a while in Montana, but he kept going further West and had told them that it wasn't until he got to Grisdale that he found what he had been looking for.

Before they left, we had a service for him. Just about everyone from camp showed up. After the prayers and tributes, while drinking coffee in the reception room at the same little church where we had said farewell to Jed, I went up to Sprint and told him some of the details of how I obtained my father's accident report and read how he was there when my father died.

"I knew your father well," he told me. "He was a good man." But Sprint didn't offer any details.

"Did Crank or you tell him to cut the corners before he went up that tree," I asked him bluntly.

"I didn't. But I wasn't there when he started climbing it, either."

"Why not? Where were you?"

"Crank had sent me up to the road to get the other set of climbing gear in case your father got stuck and needed help. By the time I got back, he was already 30 feet in the air cutting off branches."

While I was trying to think of something more to say or ask, Sprint resumed talking.

"I know what you are thinking. I've always wondered about it, too. After it was over, I asked Crank if he had warned Clifton that the tree could pull wood if he didn't cut the corners and what might happen to him if it did. Crank didn't like me asking him that. He claimed he did, but said that your father was so anxious to prove that he could climb that he didn't listen to instructions. That was partially true, but I always thought of your dad as an intelligent man. He had survived fighting in a war. If Crank actually gave him those instructions, I do not know, and to be honest I have always had my doubts. But it wasn't all Crank's fault. I was there, too."

"Yeah but you weren't there when he strapped on the spurs and belt and wrapped the climbing rope around the tree. You don't know what Crank said or didn't say to him."

"That's true, but my conscience has bothered me ever since. Had I only yelled up to him to remember to cut the corners before he started to saw the top off, he might still be alive."

"It wasn't your fault, Sprint. I don't blame you for the accident."

"Thanks. I appreciate that."

In the story I have held onto for so many years, Crank didn't choose to tell my father all he should about topping a tree. And to be honest, I have never felt much guilt about killing him. It's nothing I am happy about nor did it redeem my father's death or those of Bob and Ruby, but forgiving him has always seemed pointless to me. Perhaps just recognizing our karma during one lifetime will help us get rid of it in the next one. I hope so. That whole concept is not much different than the Christian belief of confession, redemption and forgiveness, and couched in those terms I still have a long ways to go.

The man who shot Spike was the only person charged with a crime, but it was quickly reduced from second-degree murder to assault with a deadly weapon and he was sentenced to just a year in jail. With J.T. Brown's help, Snow and I were exonerated of any wrongdoing long before the faller's trial. It took J.T. several months though to secure our rights to the treasure. I had already left the country and returned by the time that happened. Brown took a healthy chunk for himself and said it would help defend witless fools who didn't have a dime. We also gave shares to Spike's kid and Bob's parents. I actually passed on most of my cut and spread it out between the other parties. I only kept a fancy coin collection to pull out once in a while and jingle in my hands the way Bob did before he died. Snow put his share in the bank and went to Alaska after he recovered. I haven't spoken or heard from him in years, but he still lives.

In late February, as soon as I was free to go, I went to Mexico. That wasn't a good time. I drank a lot and made an ass out of myself almost nightly in the bars in Puerto Vallarta. My mother stayed clear of the place, but she had lots of friends in town, including the chief of police, and they were probably giving her reports. Towards the end of winter, my cousin Kip showed up. That was a big surprise. His fiancé and some friends were going to join him the next day but he said he came down early to talk to me. He asked if I was interested in going back to Grisdale to become a siderod so I could learn the management side of the timber business. The family was going to run Grisdale only four more years then shut it down and start logging the second growth on their private land. They wanted me to help run the second growth operation.

We had this conversation while drinking tequila under a palapa at the Playa del Sol, and I almost fell out of my chair. The idea was so outrageous I started laughing but I caught myself and for once didn't put my foot in my mouth or burn a bridge. The past couple of weeks I had been hearing the echo of chainsaws. I didn't want to admit it, but like Quiet Bob, I could feel them logging without me. It was crazy. I couldn't help it. During my stay in Vallarta, I had been telling myself I was going to go deeper into Central and South America, but to be honest I didn't know what I was going to do while traveling other than drink and feel sorry for myself. It then occurred to me what I really wanted. "I tell you what," I told Kip. "I don't want to be a siderod right now. I'm not ready for that. I want my friend's old job. I want to be the hooktender on Tower 20. I want to see if I can do half as good of a job as he did. Let me try it for a couple of years and then see how I feel about the other stuff."

"Okay," he said. He didn't hesitate a second, and to this day I don't know if he was serious about the bigger offer or just wise and skilled at a young age at reading guys like me. However, I will always be grateful he and my uncles reached out like that. For the first time ever, I felt like a full member of that branch of the family, and suddenly, I was happy. Not so much for the family stuff but because I was still a logger. I flew north the next day and was back at camp the following one. I didn't live in Bunkhouse 11 very long. It would never be the same. Even Russ was gone. He had married the bookkeeper over the winter, was living in Shelton with her and riding the town bus. I rented a place on

Lake Nahwatzel, rode the bus with him and hooked on Tower 20 until they closed camp in 1985. That was when I quit the family business. I was an old growth logger and any fool could see the days when I could practice my vocation were about over. That's when I finally went south to the Amazon, not to help cut it down, but to see the jungle.

Epilogue

A month after I returned to my home in Argentina, I received an email from Lorraine Goodwell. In it she told me that as I suspected, they had found dried semen in a pair of Ruby's undies at the bottom of her laundry bin, and their DNA analysis of the mucus I had given them confirmed that it, the semen not the underwear, belonged to me. However, since it was obvious from the progression of clothes above the panties that they had been thrown into the hamper several days before Ruby was murdered, Grays Harbor County was no longer going to follow that avenue of the investigation. She also told me that no other samples of semen had been found in or on Ruby's clothing, linen, living quarters or body, and that they had found no other evidence or heard any credible story that Ruby had had sex with anyone else at Grisdale other than Quiet Bob and me. She didn't explain why she told me that or if she knew it would be important to me, but it was, since it dissolved a perception that had been tainting my memories of Ruby forever. It also provided me an example of how life is not always the illusion we make it. In my reply, I thanked Lorraine for this information, wished her well, and told her that if she ever figured out who killed Ruby to please let me know.

El fin

About the Author

Dave Rowan is from Seattle. He has a degree in English from the University of Puget Sound, where he also played football, and a degree in Civil Engineering from the University of Washington. In between going to college, he worked in the woods for nine years as a logger on the Olympic Peninsula. Dave penned the first draft of *Loggers Don't Make Love* in 1980/81 and finished the final draft in 2020 after retiring from Seattle City Light.

The author in 1976.

About Cirque Press

Cirque Press grew out of *Cirque*, a literary journal established in 2009 by Michael Burwell, as a vehicle for the publication of writers and artists of the North Pacific Rim. This region is broadly defined as reaching north from Oregon to the Yukon Territory and south through Alaska to Hawaii – and west to the Russian Far East. Sandra Kleven joined *Cirque* in 2012 working as a partner with Burwell.

Our contributors are widely published in an array of journals. Their writing is significant. It is personal. It is strong. It draws on these regions in ways that add to the culture of places.

We felt that the works of individual writers could be lost if it were to remain scattered across the literary landscape. Therefore, we established a press to collect these writing efforts. Cirque Press seeks to gather the work of our contributors into book form where it can be experienced coherently as statement, observation, and artistry.

Sandra Kleven – Michael Burwell, publishers and editors
www.cirquejournal.com

Books From Cirque Press

Apportioning the Light by Karen Tschannen (2018)

The Lure of Impermanence by Carey Taylor (2018)

Echolocation by Kristin Berger (2018)

Like Painted Kites & Collected Works by Clifton Bates (2019)

Athabaskan Fractal: Poems of the Far North by Karla Linn Merrifield (2019)

Holy Ghost Town by Tim Sherry (2019)

Drunk on Love: Twelve Stories to Savor Responsibly by Kerry Dean Feldman (2019)

Wide Open Eyes: Surfacing from Vietnam by Paul Kirk Haeder (2020)

Silty Water People by Vivian Faith Prescott (2020)

Life Revised by Leah Stenson (2020)

Oasis Earth: Planet in Peril by Rick Steiner (2020)

The Way to Gaamaak Cove by Doug Pope (2020)

Loggers Don't Make Love by Dave Rowan (2020)

The Dream That Is Childhood by Sandra Wassilie (2020)

Seward Soundboard by Sean Ulman (2020)

The Fox Boy Gretchen Brinck (2020)

More Praise for *Loggers Don't Make Love*

Knowing just enough about lumber and logging for my own trade, which is lumber brokering, I had a limited understanding of what logging involved. *Loggers Don't Make Love* clarified that for me—*and then some*—throwing in intense human interactions in close quarters. Dave Rowan offers a rugged and gritty story about men and a few unforgettable women who work at a logging camp in Washington State in what is considered one of the most dangerous jobs there is. The novel includes an intriguing murder mystery. A love story that floats through the complex technology of logging revved up my interest. I liked this novel.

—Ray Haroldson, President, Haroldson Group International

CPSIA information can be obtained
at www.ICGtesting.com
Printed in the USA
LVHW110806130121
676356LV00003B/330